⫸ **W9-BZH-906**

Leaves high overhead, turning and shaking in the wind, let the light cascade down in the intermittent showers, immersing us in gold and amber, losing us in shadow. Georgie let go of my hand and said, "Sit here. I'll give you a present."

She stood at the back of the pool, motionless. She said, "It takes a while for your eyes to adjust."

I could remember. The frogs were gold, like the light, and they had small black spots, like the shadow. Until your eyes grew accustomed, they blended into their surroundings, invisible. Unless one of them moved. But they too would freeze, as motionless as Georgie. As motionless as I. I remembered. When Georgie and Dito came upon me that distant summer day, I had just caught a frog. I had caught it for her and then, as if the wishing in my mind had conjured her, there she had been, high on her white horse, smiling.

Georgie broke into my reverie saying, "Here's a present. I owe you one. You probably don't remember." She handed me a golden frog, descendant I was sure, of the one I had once given her.

For Joan McCullough Oman,
my real life cousin in Panama.

Murder
IS GERMANE
A BRIGID DONOVAN MYSTERY
BY KAREN SAUM

The Naiad Press, Inc.
1991

Copyright © 1991 by Karen Saum

All rights reserved. No part of this book may be reproduced or transmitted in any form or by any means, electronic or mechanical, including photocopying, without permission in writing from the publisher.

Printed in the United States of America on acid-free paper
First Edition

Edited by Katherine V. Forrest
Cover design by Pat Tong and Bonnie Liss
    (Phoenix Graphics)
Typeset by Sandi Stancil

Library of Congress Cataloging-in-Publication Data

Saum, Karen, 1935–
    Murder is germane : a Brigid Donovan mystery / by Karen
    Saum.
        p.   cm.
    ISBN 0-941483-98-3 : $8.95
    I. Title.
PS3569.A7887M6   1991
813'.54--dc20   91-22262
                                                                      CIP

Chapter 1

Three months ago, on the phone, Mother said, "Brigid, why don't you come with me on this cruise. Just the transit of the Canal. We'll fly down and stay with Susan. To celebrate the Seventy-Fifth Anniversary. You know."

The Anniversary she meant was the opening of the Panama Canal. Her dad had worked on its construction. In fact, she was born in a construction camp, Gorgona, flooded now, under Gatun Lake and part of the Canal. Where I was born is also gone. On Limon Bay, in Cristobal. That's the Atlantic Side.

On the phone I said, "Yeah. I'd love to go."

Then she added, "Lucho's band is playing."

And, too late, I remembered Cotillion classes in Panama City and the partner I called Jerkey, because his name rhymed with Jerkey, and because he was. Mother says the reason I called him Jerkey is I was a brat. Maybe so.

El Valle, once a volcano, has a kidney-shaped floor completely surrounded by jungle-clad mountains. At the end of our transit of the Canal, several of us went there. Mother and I, my cousin, Susan Arosemena, who still lives in Panama, and three fellows on the cruise, Bruce McAntee, Bobby Jardin, and Tony Brown. The six of us had two things in common: a diploma from Cristobal High School, and, once upon a time, a weekend home in El Valle in the interior of Panama. On the strength of these connections, we had decided during the shipboard party the night before to spend two days together for Auld Lang Syne.

Bruce McAntee, like my cousin Susan Arosemena, was Class of '67. To me they would have passed for this year's crop of graduates. But I've noticed recently that anyone under forty looks dewy. Too, they had been chosen Best Athlete for the Zonian, Cristobal High School's Year Book, and they probably still run a couple marathons a year. Not so Bobby Jardin. He looked even more tired than I felt, his eyes sunk in mournful blue hollows shadowed by thickets of tangled eyebrows. He had confided to me the night before that the apartment above his pharmacy in Blue Hill, Maine, had a guest room waiting for me. "Yeah," I said and left in search of the Ladies.

2

The last of our crew, Tony Brown, in his early twenties and really a baby, was the son of Dito Brown, the big football hero of my girlhood. Mother says I was in love with Dito. Who I was in love with was Dito's sister, Georgie. It isn't surprising Mother didn't know. At twelve, I didn't either.

The hotel in El Valle where we stayed, long and low with red tiled roof, creamy stucco walls and purple bougainvillea everywhere, was the big one at the base of Las Tres Hermanas, the highest of the circling mountains. Except for a couple of macaws, the six of us were the only inhabitants of the wide veranda. It was a bad year for tourists, that fall of 1989. Panama's dictator, Noriega, had had a falling out with his former pal, George Bush, and that made the tourists nervous.

Rocking on the veranda, my five companions were busy trying, with frozen daiquiris, to recapture the mood of the night before. I had never had the mood, and my drink was frozen orange juice. What I needed wasn't Auld Lang Syne but a meeting. I wondered, sour as the lime thoughtfully stuck on the rim of my glass, whether AA had come to the valley.

"Where's Georgie these days?" I asked Tony Brown. Georgie Hendryks. My old love, Tony's aunt.

Tony said, "In Cartagena."

"She still have her place here?" I asked, remembering the summer when I was twelve and had staked it out, my horse tethered nearby. With my binoculars trained for hours on the house I would lie, hidden, hoping to catch a glimpse of her. Not knowing why I was acting so crazy. Knowing only that I had to.

Tony said she did.

3

Mother said, "Oh, does she? I thought she lived in Cartagena now."

"Well, she does," Tony agreed. "She runs the *fincas* now Orlando's gone."

Orlando Hendryks, legendary patriarch of a Columbian family with as many branches as it had plantations. Orlando, in return for a handsome dowry, had extracted the promise that his first grandchild would be given the surname Hendryks. *In utero,* the child had been called Orlandito, or just Dito. At birth, they thought it prudent to change her name to Georgina.

Tony giggled. "Georgie's got the whole enchilada."

I hadn't seen Tony since he was two, some twenty years before. He was an *enfant terrible* then, and he didn't seem to have changed. I couldn't remember the giggle.

Bruce said, "Think we could go up there?" He smoothed the springing cowlick on the crown of his head. In the dusk he looked sixteen. "I used to think she had the best view in the valley when I was a kid."

"When was that, yesterday?" I said, but no one laughed. "Yeah. Let's go. I would really like to."

Bobby Jardin groaned. "Count me out!" he said brusquely. The half-moon bay of skin above his brow glowed briefly red, catching, as he rose, the last vermilion rays of the setting sun.

"Oh, come with us, Bobby!" said Mother.

"For Christ's sake, Vera, would you stop calling me Bobby! My name is Robert." He strode away toward the pool.

"What got into him?" Mother asked no one in particular.

4

And no one responded. Except Tony. He giggled.

Other than seeming smaller, Georgie's house was much as I remembered it. Flowing stucco curves over doors and windows, wrought iron vines and flowers in every aperture. On the roof, tiles of dull red brick, and underfoot gleaming tiles of ceramic. Bruce McAntee was right: the view across the tranquil valley was still superb. In the end, he and I had gone alone. We had never met before that week, though it seemed to me I had known him forever. Susan once had written ecstatic letters about him, and Mother always included him in her gossip about former Zonians. When he suggested we walk to Georgie's, I agreed with the proviso that he match his pace to mine. "I haven't run a marathon . . . recently," I said, and changed the subject when he asked my time.

Sitting on Georgie's back porch looking across to La Princessa Dormida, Bruce asked, "Did you know Georgie well?"

"I hardly knew her at all. She was a lot older than I."

In the middle distance I could see the roof of the Dutchman's farm where, that summer of infatuation, I went daily for eggs, hoping to catch sight of Georgie. After a week or so, Mother had said, "Brigid! We have enough eggs to feed an army. No more eggs!" That's when I began my stake-out.

"She must be quite a lady," Bruce said.

"What makes you say that?" I asked.

"Well, the Hendryks family has a lot of property. If she's running it . . ."

I said, "Yeah."

My memory of Georgie was that she was quite a

5

lady. Not because of any property she managed, however. But because she was beautiful and blonde. Because she drove a lime-green convertible and rode a white stallion. Because her saddle was English and she jumped fences. In my memory, Georgie Hendryks was twenty-four and she always would be. For me, she was the definition of glamour, and she would always be that, also.

"How old is she?" asked Bruce.

Good question. If she was twelve years older than I, it would make her, unimaginably, closer to Mother's age than mine. It would make her not Georgie Hendryks.

"I'm sorry," said Bruce, embarrassed. He began to punish his cowlick. "I didn't mean to pry."

"Oh. No problem. I'm fifty-four, so that would make Georgie sixty-six. That's young. These days."

Young? Maybe. But glamorous? No. Not glamorous.

Then I remembered, when I was Bruce's age, how glamorous Isak Dinesen had seemed, eating oysters and sipping champagne. I remembered Piaf, belting out her songs in Paris and marrying ever-younger men. I remembered Ingrid Bergman. I'd fallen in love with Ingrid Bergman the summer I fell in love with Georgie Hendryks. I had remained faithful to them both, in my fashion, all my life.

"I sure would like to see her again," I heard myself say, and knew, by the twist of my gut, that I meant it.

Walking back to the hotel, Bruce asked what I knew about the missing man from Maine, Chester Brown.

6

"Not much," I said. "Other than he was an INS man." Immigration and Naturalization Service. "I live in Greenville. He was from somewhere on the coast."

"Blue Hill," said Bruce.

"Right. Bobby lives in Blue Hill, doesn't he? Bobby mentioned he knew him."

"I think we better call him Robert."

I laughed. "Ask Robert, then, about him."

Bruce said, "Oh, it's not important." Then he said, "I read your book, by the way. You solved a crime, a murder, committed maybe fifty years ago?"

"Yes," I said.

"It was good."

"Thanks."

"You should look into this disappearance."

"Chester Brown's?"

"Yes. He was also known as Carlos Pardo. He had a sister. Name of Maria."

Ours was the only party in the hotel dining room that evening. The mist of a *bajareque* made the night air moist and cool. Robert Jardin sat by me. He must have slept while Bruce and I toiled our way up to Georgie Hendryks'. The hollows of his eyes appeared less bosky, and he seemed to have recovered his good humor. Everyone called him Robert. Even Mother.

After dinner, sipping a brandy, he said, "By the way, Brigid, I read your book."

"Oh yeah?" I said.

He said, "Clever detective work."

7

"Thanks."

"You know, you should look into the disappearance of that Chester Brown."

"Aka Carlos Pardo."

"So you know about it."

"A little," said I.

"Well, when you get back to Maine. If you're interested. Think about it. I might be able to help. It happened in Blue Hill, you know. Where I live. Your mother says you live up in the boonies."

"Greenville."

"Right. It's not that far. Three hours maybe. You're welcome to stay with me, you know."

"Yeah. Right. Above your drugstore."

His right eyebrow rose. "I beg your pardon? Oh, you mean my pharmacy."

By then everyone seemed to have recaptured the spirit of Auld Lang Syne that had eluded them during the day.

Everyone but me. I went to bed with a book I had brought. Brought wrapped in a plain brown cover. *Lesbian Nuns: Breaking Silence.* Vanity. I was in it.

Chapter 2

I know this nun. Her name is Sister Pat. Not a Lesbian Nun. More's the pity. I wouldn't mind breaking Sr. Pat's silence with her.

A year or so ago I had helped clear up a serious problem at the convent, a novice who had disappeared. A novice whose mother and father had been brutally murdered.

I wasn't back in Greenville twenty-four hours when Sr. Pat called. She sounded upset.

"How was Panama," she said and stuff like that.

Then she said, "You're probably tired and glad to be home."

I said, "Yeah."

She said, "How's Nell?"

Nell's my landlady.

Then Pat said, "How's Jackie?"

"You want to talk to them?" I asked. "They could tell you better than I."

I could hear Pat sigh, a lovely sound in my ear. She has gorgeous red hair she keeps copper bright with frequent henna rinses. With my eyes closed I thought I could see it glowing. It might have been the afterglow of the setting sun I saw.

Pat said, "Is there any chance you could come for a visit? You could stay in Gen's old room," she added, as if that might entice me.

Gen's old room wouldn't entice a field mouse. It's about six by six with a built-in cot, a built-in desk, and room enough left over to turn around in, if you're slender and move slow.

Three nuns, Sr. Pat, Sr. Barnabas and Sr. Genevieve, had built the convent. They used scrap lumber and donated windows. The nuns live in a big tarpaper building with a bambrel roof. It looks like a barn. A *Tobacco Road* barn. At the end of a cloistered walk, the animals, a cow, two goats and some laying hens, live in a gabled, board-and-batten building. It looks like a house. The nuns make a living by selling goat's milk cheese and by blackmail. Pat makes the cheese, and Sr. Barnabas — or Barney — does the blackmail.

"Gen's room," I repeated, without enthusiasm.

"I put a dormer in," said Pat. "It's got a lot more

light now. Makes it seem bigger. It's really pretty nice."

She sighed in my ear again. I remembered: Gen's old room is next door to Pat's. Maybe Pat would sigh in the night if I stayed.

Pat said, "I really wish you'd come, Brigid."

October is my favorite month in Maine. The days are warm and sunny, but no bugs, and the nights are cool enough to want a fire. Best of all, the world is ablaze with color. I enjoyed the ride down from Greenville to the coast.

Supper in the convent was just for Pat and me. She and Barney were now the only residents. We had goat's milk cheese with herbs, fresh mint tea, and warm milk with honey. Except for the grain in the dark rye bread, Pat had produced it all. I said, "So you like raising bees."

She said, "I like the honey part of it." We sat on benches near the wood cook stove.

"I'm afraid Barney may be in over her head," said Pat.

"Barney?" I may have snorted; I know Pat smiled.

My opinion of Barney: If she squared off with Lucifer, next day he'd be searching the Want Ads for a job.

"I know you don't like her," said Pat.

"What are you afraid of?" I asked.

"Well," said Pat, "she's got herself mixed up with some religious community up the coast. Remember

11

last year, that INS man, Chester Brown, he disappeared."

"Yeah. I remember."

"Well, it's that community. You know, they take in refugees. Help them get across the border. Into Canada?"

I nodded. I did know. Something else I knew was that Sr. Barnabas wasn't guilty of being a Good Samaritan. Breaking the law by transporting refugees was not what had worried Sr. Pat, worried her into complete silence as she sat across from me nibbling at her thumbnail. There was a time when I would have started to make suggestions to fill the silence, offering a sort of multiple choice of problems for Pat to pick from. To rescue her from discomfort, to save her from the burden of responsibility to explain. A day at a time I had gotten to the point where I could wait the silence out. Eventually Pat said, "What I'm worried about is Barney has got her hands on some extra cash again."

This community, Pat told me, where Barney had taken to hanging out, was called Monte Cassino. It had been around for about twenty years. Not church-connected, but quasi-religious. Before it became a sanctuary for refugees, there had been reports from time to time of people being cured there by the founder/leader, a woman called Sr. Clara.

"Sr. Clara?" I asked. "You said it wasn't religious."

"It's not," Pat asserted. "Oh, I don't really know," she amended. "My Formation Director suggests strongly that I give the place a wide berth. Apparently this Sr. Clara and another nun, Sr.

12

Benedict, were novices together. Carmelites. The rumor is, Clara was expelled and Benedict went with her. So they're both out of order. But Benedict's mother — this is twenty years ago, so the mother must be getting up there — anyway, she backed them financially. I think the mother may be one of the Grace family. Central America? She's got lots of money anyhow. But the community never had much. I mean, they were really poor."

She looked around her appraisingly, surprising me: I had always thought Pat did not see the broken down furniture, the exposed insulation, the stains in the carpet that she had salvaged from the dump. I had thought Pat always mistook the ideal she strove for as the reality she was immersed in.

"Oh, I see it, Brigid," she said. "I just don't dwell on it."

The light from the kerosene lamp was dim, but I think she blushed.

"Even though they were poor, the folks at Monte Cassino always took people in. Homeless people, people from prison. Then the refugees from El Salvador and Guatemala. Down around Blue Hill the people talk about Clara like she's Mother Theresa."

Pat grimaced her disapproval, then continued, "But all of a sudden, about the time Chester Brown disappeared, they had all this money. How I know is, that's when Barney got interested in them. They started paying their bills in town, and they started building. You know, shelters for the homeless and stuff like that. But a lot of it. I mean it's like the Patten Corporation, the scale of development. And the planning board is letting them, which is really weird."

There was more, but Pat wasn't ready to tell me. She took my cup and hers and rinsed them at the long slate sink, pumping water from a little red hand pump. It squealed discontentedly.

"Needs oil," I said.

"I know," she replied. She turned toward me. Her hair caught light from the lamp and held it. A willing prisoner, for it played happily there. She wore jeans and a plaid work shirt. I had spent the night with her once before. At night she wears flannel pajamas.

"Brigid, that's the other thing. Why I called. Barney says we're getting running water. Brigid, do you know how much it will cost to bring in electricity?"

I had a good idea. And it was a lot. The road into the convent through the woods is the better part of a mile. Once upon a time, Barney leaned on me to provide the cash to make the road accessible year round. She thought I might pay to hide the fact I'm a lesbian. But it's only books I hide inside a plain brown cover. And I only do that for my mother.

After supper I helped with the chores and we turned in early. If Pat sighed in the night, it wasn't in my ear and I didn't hear her. When I got up at six, Pat was already in the barn milking. She had a fire going and a pot of coffee keeping warm at the back of the cook stove. I took her out a cup. Over breakfast, dark rye bread with goat's milk cheese and scrambled eggs fresh from the nest, she explained my day to me.

"On Saturdays, people — volunteers — go out to

Monte Cassino and help out. I want you to go. In the evening, at five-thirty, they have worship service and then supper."

"Worship service?" I repeated.

"Yes," she said.

"What kind of worship service?"

"Oh, Brigid. Don't be difficult."

"I'm not being difficult," I pointed out, "I just want to know what they do. Do they sacrifice chickens to a Mayan god? For instance."

"Brigid! Don't be ridiculous."

"Don't be ridiculous. That must mean they go in for a little cannibalism."

"Brigid, I hate to have to tell you this, but the reason you get so irritable is you are longing to come back to the fold."

I let it pass, realizing I should never have gotten into it in the first place. I do not want to return to the fold. The fold, as I had experienced it, felt more like a crease, and I damn near smothered in it. But neither do I want this nagging resentment of the Church that has dogged me ever since I left it. I said, "So, is it Mass?"

"If there's a priest there, yes. But usually there isn't and they just improvise. They read some Scripture, recite a poem, sing a song. Some of the people can't read, so they speak from their heart instead of from a book. I was moved."

"Barney won't be there?" I asked.

Pat shook her head.

I thought about it a while in silence. Then I said, "What do I say when I get there? Hello, my name is Brigid Donovan and I want to know if

15

Barney is blackmailing you because you run drugs? And the reason I want to know is, Barney's partner, Sr. Pat, draws a line at drugs."

"Brigid Donovan! That's plain mean."

She was right. It was mean. But her precious cloisters connecting the house to the barn had been built with some New York money Barney had volunteered to launder, a fact I had uncovered in a case I had recently investigated. Like socks, the money had been lost in the wash.

"I'm sorry," I said, trying to sound contrite.

"You're not sorry at all!" Then she said, "You don't have to explain yourself at Monte Cassino. People just come and they put them to work. You might shingle, or split wood. Whatever needs doing. Brigid, please. I want to know what's going on out there."

"What does Barney say is going on?"

Pat's face hardened. "Barney says they have the true spirit and faith. Whatever that means," she added bitterly.

If it had been anyone else, I would have said she was jealous.

"Take this with you," she said, pushing a paper bag across the table at me. "Your donation for supper — a jar of honey and a loaf of bread. It's a case of loaves and fishes," she said, her voice acid enough to curdle the milk in the pitcher. "According to Barney, every Saturday night at six a miracle occurs. And it's not even prime time."

She *was* jealous! Amazing.

"Then what?" I asked.

"Would you mind coming back here? To tell me what you find out?"

Who knows? Tonight she might sigh in my ear. I said, "Sure. Why not."

"One more thing," said Pat. "It's an island."

"Oh, right! How do I . . ."

"Let's look at the tides," she said.

At low tide you could walk to the island on a gravel spit. We discovered I could go across between about ten in the morning and one in the afternoon.

"I'm not spending the night there," I said.

"You better by God not spend the night there," she assured me. "You can row back. Just don't take your car across. Then you would be stuck."

When I arrived at Monte Cassino an hour later, the woman of my dreams was there waiting at the shore for me. Tall, with long red hair pulled back in a ponytail, she was dressed for the woods in jeans, a plaid lumber jacket, and boots. She was younger than I, but these days, who isn't. Maybe in her early forties.

"Brigid Donovan," I said and offered her my hand.

She took it. "Maria Papandreou," she said. Then she said, "*The* Brigid Donovan? Am I ever glad to meet you."

She seemed to like my hand especially. At least, she kept hanging on to it.

She said, "Maybe you could help me."

I said, "Yeah. Maybe so."

She said, "I liked your book. Maybe you could help me find out what happened to Carlos Pardo. Also known as . . ."

"Chester Brown."

"Oh! Is that why you're here then?"

"Maybe," I said. "Maybe."

I stuck with Maria all day. We worked on firewood. There were three of us at it: Maria, Sr. Clara and me. Clara I never saw, not until evening. I heard her, though. She milled around in the woods dropping trees, Maria and I following after. Maria four-footed with a Stihl chainsaw, while I lopped branches and bundled the sticks, tidying up after the two of them.

I mentioned that Sr. Pat's convent looked like *Tobacco Road.* So did Monte Cassino. The island was maybe four hundred acres, most of it woods. Maria had said there was a cedar bog. A ridge, called Soper's Ridge, was where we cut that afternoon. It overlooked Frenchman's Bay, and protected the community from bad weather. The community consisted of a dozen or so shacks, some partially shingled, others just tarpapered, and a couple of out-houses and a barn. Bedraggled is how it looked. And raw. As Pat said, there was a lot of construction going on and nothing seemed finished, even buildings that had been there for a while: for instance, the out-house Maria directed me to had no roof. I wondered about using it in a snowstorm, or a thundershower.

At one o'clock we broke for lunch — a kettle of popcorn with nutritional yeast and soy sauce instead of salt. It wasn't bad, but I was glad I had thought to bring along a bag of apples, which I shared. There were six or seven volunteers, local folk it seemed, including a sheriff by the name of Danny. We all introduced ourselves before the service, which, thank God, was not Mass. No priest on hand to make the bread into Jesus. The bread was moldy, though, so I declined it anyway.

Sr. Clara was an impressive figure of a woman. She was dressed in blue denim down to her shoes, plus a black and white bandanna she wore like a coif so that all you could see of her hair was a narrow strip, the color of brick, above her forehead. She didn't talk much. In fact, except for mumbling "My name is Sr. Clara" when we went around introducing ourselves, I didn't hear her say a word. She kept her head down all through worship. The only feature I got a good look at was this mole up where the bridge of her nose began, like a third eye. The little veins feeding it seemed to glow and pulsate all through Mass. If I were her, I'd have it looked at. I mentioned it to Maria afterward. Maria just laughed. She said, "Oh, it does that when Clara meditates."

When she meditates?

At five o'clock when we stopped work, Maria took me down the hill to an octagonal shack she called the Immaculate Conception. Immaculate it wasn't, although the shape was womb-like. There, Maria told me, was the last place anyone had seen Chester Brown.

"Alive," I said idly, just filling in the blank.

"Well, not really," said Maria, then she turned and started back up the hill. So I didn't have a

chance to ask her what she meant. It's a hill you
don't ask questions on. At the top, Ingrid Bergman
stood waiting for us. So I didn't ask then either.

Bergman said, "What were you doing at
Immaculate Conception?"

"Benedict," Maria said, "this is Brigid, she came
to volunteer for the day. I was showing her the
community." To me she said, "Brigid, Sr. Benedict.
She and Clara founded Monte Cassino. Benedict lives
in Immaculate Conception."

I said, "Oh."

Sr. Benedict said nothing more and, brushing
past us, headed down the hill.

"She always that friendly?" I asked.

But Maria seemed not to have heard.

The building where we gathered for worship and
to eat was called Trinity. There were maybe fifteen
of us altogether. Introductions hardly helped me to
sort out who were volunteers and who were
residents. If I hadn't heard of Sr. Clara, I wouldn't
even have caught her name, let alone known who
she was.

From Sr. Pat's point of view, my visit seemed to
have been a failure. And as for me, I would have
done better staying at home and getting in my own
wood for winter. Furthermore, if this day was typical
of Monte Cassino — no mingling, hardly any
conversation — coming back again wouldn't do any
good either. Besides, I didn't see what there could be
in this dilapidated place to attract Sr. Pat's
blackmailing partner, Sr. Barnabas. Nor had I seen
anything to suggest what or who had made Pat
jealous. The loaves-and-fishes scene was nothing to
write home about. Only Pat's bread and honey

looked edible. The unappetizing casseroles I saw laid out on the table made me decide to leave right after the service. I thought I'd stop at Duffy's Restaurant for supper.

These were the thoughts that occupied my mind while the rest of the congregation got high on Jesus. With the last of "Amazing Grace" echoing in my ears, I approached Maria.

"How do you get off this place?" I asked her.

"Oh stay for dinner," she said.

"Actually," I lied, "I'm supposed to meet someone at Duffy's for dinner. At six-thirty," I improvised to establish a sense of urgency.

"It's nearly that now," said Maria.

"I know."

"Well, then," she said, "I should come with you."

"No need to do that," I said. "If you'll just explain the ropes. I'm sure I can manage."

But Maria wasn't listening. She was looking for someone and not finding her. Only Sr. Clara had gone. I had seen her leave as they sang, "to save a wretch like me," when everyone else had their eyes closed.

"Sr. Clara left," I said.

Maria turned to me, surprised. Her eyes narrowed. "Oh," she said. "Sherlock Holmes. Can I be Watson?"

"I'm sure that would be interesting," said I. "But I'm not working on a case."

"Let me take you to dinner then, at Duffy's. Maybe I can get you to work on one for me."

"I don't think so."

"Oh, right. You're meeting someone else."

"Don't worry about that," I said ambiguously.

21

We walked down to the shore in the waning light. There, tied to a rope running from shore to shore, was a little dinghy. Fiddling with an oarlock was Sr. Clara. Ignoring me, she said to Maria, "I didn't expect you today."

Maria said, "Clara, you haven't met my friend Brigid. She and I were working behind you today, clearing brush."

Clara turned and thrust her hand at me. I took it and held it. The palm felt warm and crusty with calluses. It felt strong and comforting.

Clara thrust her clear brown eyes into mine. I took them, too, and held them. Her eyes were deeper than fathoms, with an undertow I was helpless to resist.

She said, "Brigid. Welcome. We've been waiting for you."

I said, "Oh yeah?"

Maria said, "You coming, Brigid? It's already after six, you know."

Reluctantly I rescued my eyes and returned Clara's hand to her. I climbed into the dinghy.

Clara said, "Will you come again? Brigid?"

I said, "Yeah. No problem." Without looking back, I said, "Next Saturday."

I think Maria was laughing. But it was too dark to see, so I wasn't sure.

I got back to the convent a little past eight. Pat took one look at me walking in the door and cried out, "Oh, sugar! I don't believe it! Brigid, not you too."

"What do you mean?" I said.

But I knew what she meant. What I didn't know was how she could tell.

"You know perfectly well what I mean," said Pat. "It's written all over your face. I'm going to bed."

One day at a time, I've learned that the only way to stay sober is to stay honest. I should have said to Pat, "Yes, I do know what you mean. Sr. Clara bowled me over. So what."

But I couldn't do it. To this day I have trouble coming to terms with the look Sr. Clara and I exchanged that evening on the shore of Monte Cassino. There was a quality of conspiracy in it, of my having been admitted to some private place known only to us. That the look was seductive and highly erotic I denied for months, with consequences far-ranging and destructive.

"Don't you want to know about my day?" I asked.

"I doubt," Pat flung over her shoulder as she headed for the ladder leading upstairs, "I'd find out anything I don't already know."

Guilt made me huffy. "Suit yourself!" I said. "Goodnight!"

All but her feet had disappeared through the hole in the floor before Pat hesitated. Slowly she backed down the ladder. She said, "Brigid, I'm sorry. What you think of Sr. Clara is your own business. Did you enjoy your day at Monte Cassino?"

"Not much," I told her. I asked if she'd ever been out there.

"Once," she said. She offered me tea, like a peace pipe. I accepted.

We sat at the picnic table across from one

another with tea and bread and honey spread between us, a homely demilitarized zone.

After some desultory conversation, I asked what she knew about the missing INS man, Chester Brown.

"Do you think," I asked, "there could be a connection between Brown's disappearance and Barney's interest in Monte Cassino?"

"Like drugs you mean? That seemed to be what the newspapers were driving at when it happened."

"If you're suggesting what I think you're suggesting," I said, "I think you're all wet."

Pat looked surprised at my tone. I couldn't blame her.

"And what am I suggesting, Brigid?" she asked.

"I'm not going to talk about it," I said.

"Deny it all you want," she invited. "But if Chester Brown staged his disappearance in order to protect Monte Cassino as the distribution point for drugs, that would account for a lot. It would account for their prosperity, it would account for —"

I cut her off. "That's preposterous."

"Preposterous?"

Pat had been breaking off pieces of bread and rolling them into pellets. She had a mound of this ammunition piled by her plate. I began to arm myself with the heel of the loaf. In case our war of nerves turned hot.

"Why preposterous?" she demanded. "You're so sure Barney's blackmailing someone — then who? And why?"

Good questions. But I didn't want to hear them.

"Don't be so paranoid," I snapped. "They're not running drugs at Monte Cassino."

"You're there for six hours and you know that?"

"Yes!" I said.

"How?"

"It's just obvious. That's all. It's not that kind of place."

"Not that kind of place," she mocked. "What you mean is your precious Santa Clara —"

Again I cut her off. "What the hell is wrong with you! *Santa* Clara? Come on!"

Her eyes dulled. "You're right," she said. "I'm sorry. What you think of Clara is your business." She rose from the table. "But I'm tired, and I have to be up in a few hours to milk. I want to thank you for coming. I really appreciate it. If I don't see you in the morning, have a safe trip. And say hello to Nell for me."

"Hey, wait a minute," I said, casting about in my mind for a way to hold her. "I met a woman there named Maria. Do you know her?"

Pat nodded, uninterested.

I explained about Maria's interest in Chester Brown and that she wanted me to investigate his disappearance. "She asked me to dinner tomorrow night. I said I didn't think so. But if you'd come with me, I'd go."

Like her earlier offer of tea, my invitation was to make peace, and she accepted. So Pat and I went to bed friends. Not as close friends as I would have liked. But pretty close. She brushed her cheek past mine before she turned into her cell. As I drifted off to sleep, I heard her sigh not once but several times through gaps in the rough pine boarding that separated her cot from mine.

Chapter 3

Dinner the next night was at H.O.P.E. where Maria lived with a woman named Alex. H.O.P.E.'s an ecumenical organization near the coast between Penobscot Bay and Union River Bay. My last case had brought me there and I've kept in touch over the years with one friend I made that summer. I call her my Jane Marple.

According to Sr. Pat, Maria's partner, Alex, worked as construction supervisor for the summer volunteers at H.O.P.E. What Maria mostly did was paint. "When I say paint," said Pat, "I'm talking canvas. What they thought she would paint was the chapel."

Supper turned out to be spaghetti and wine. You ask me, Alex had a long head start on the wine.

"Alex Adler!" she greeted us at the door. "One of you is the detective and the other one's the nun. But God knows which is which, and I guess it doesn't matter much. Come in and make yourselves to home. Wine?" She flourished a half gallon of Gallo in our direction.

Pat accepted a mug. I declined. Said I'd get some water at the pump. Which I did, spending some time there trying to center myself. The evening looked to be an ordeal. *One of you is the detective and the other one's a nun.* Good God!

I'd been sober a few twenty-four hours, and had pretty much stopped going to AA meetings, except for anniversaries and once in a while when I felt really bummed out. I should have been going more often, like whenever I found myself doing some "stinkin' thinkin'." Like then — my reaction to Alex. All I could see was an old woman with a drinking problem who was going to be a pain in the butt before the night was done.

Sipping my water, watching the sky turn coral, slowly, above the silhouette of pointed fir beyond the meadow, I tried to stop comparing and to identify. I succeeded all too well.

First I recognized in the rosy network of broken veins that flushed her cheeks the spurious health that glowed in mine.

Then, in Alex's careless conviviality I began to see my own capacity for drunken bonhomie.

Finally, I found lurking in the gray of her hair and the lines of her face my own old woman.

All this identification left me dizzy with revulsion. What I wanted was reassurance: Brigid Donovan like Alex Adler? No way!

When I returned, the party was in full swing. Even Pat's eyes had an unfamiliar glitter.

"We've agreed," announced Maria, "that you are to investigate the disappearance of Carlos Pardo, aka Chester Brown, and find out where Clara's getting all that money from. Here," she said, pushing a jar of wine at me, "drink to it."

Pat intercepted the jar. "I'll take it," she said. "Brigid doesn't drink. Do you, Brigid?"

"You what?" said Alex.

"Don't drink?" said Maria.

I wrested the jar from Pat and swilled the wine in one long swallow.

In my mind I did. In the pale light of dusk and reality, I said, "Yeah," and sat down. "Are we having spaghetti?"

"Are you hungry?" asked Maria.

"Famished," I replied.

"The spaghetti is not *al dente*," Maria announced, a while later, as she served it. An understatement.

"Oops!" said Alex. "I forgot the salad."

"We don't need a salad," Maria assured her.

I don't know why all this had me so up tight. Dinners with my old friend and former drinking buddy, Ed Kelly, had been every bit as drunk and disorderly and they had never bothered me.

Realizing that I found it easier to identify with that reprobate Ed than with this woman Alex amused me. Finding myself ridiculous, I turned with better humor to Alex and said, "Have you been to Monte Cassino?"

For a long moment no one spoke. I said, "Don't everyone talk at once."

Then everyone did.

The person I heard was Alex. She said, "Jesus Christ! That's like asking does Mother Theresa have tits. Yeah, I been to Monte Cassino. Santa Clara and I lived together. Three years. Seemed more like ten. Someone pass the wine."

Well? What had I thought? That Clara was some virgin waiting to be made love to by me?

My brain scoffed. But my gut knew.

"What's wrong with you?" I heard Alex ask. I hauled my derelict mind back to the table.

"Clara zapped her," Maria said in a confiding voice.

"Oh," said Alex, suddenly sober-seeming. "Poor Brigid," she said.

Poor Brigid? I said, "What are you guys talking about? I ask a simple question. I guess the answer is . . ."

"Yes," said Pat, her voice brittle.

I decided to leave. But before I could move, the door opened and a young man wearing an embroidered shirt, a Panamanian *guayabera*, appeared in the doorway. He looked exactly like Tony Brown, whom I last had seen giggling on the hotel veranda in El Valle.

"Maria," he said, "hope you don't mind dropping in like this."

"Tony! Dear God! What a surprise!" Maria exclaimed. "Come in."

She rose and embraced him. Turning to us she announced, "My cousin, Tony Hendryks. Tony's from Panama." And then she introduced us: "My friend, Alex. Brigid. Sr. Pat."

Tony nodded, dimly. He said, "Hey, I don't want to break up a party." He giggled.

"Tony," I said, "don't you remember me?"

"Sure," he said. "How ya' doin'?"

"What brings you to Maine?" I asked. But no one was home.

"Any wine?" asked Tony.

Alex brought another chair, a folding metal one, from the other room while Maria began to scrape our dinner dishes into a plastic bucket for compost. Pat and I moved closer together to make room for Tony.

It had grown quite dark outside. A candle in a wine bottle, oozing blisters of wax like a fungus, shed the only light. Tony sat beside me and twitched, as if erratic electric currents animated his extremities. He drummed an intermittent tattoo on the table top. Wired, and driving me bananas.

I said to Pat's back — she was listening to some rigmarole from Alex — "I think I'll visit my friend for a minute and then roll on home." I asked her back, "Do you want a ride with me?"

Pat said, not bothering to look around, "Sure. Call me when you're ready."

They were all of them on some other planet. Planet Alcohol. In moon orbit. Crazy. I got out of there.

My Jane Marple friend, who's confined to a wheelchair — her body is confined; her mind roams the universe — was glad to see me and commiserated on my discomforts. She offered me some apple juice, the strongest drink in her house. After half an hour of chit chat, I said, "Can I use your phone? I got a credit card."

Who I called was Bruce McAntee of the pretty muscles and unruly cowlick. In Portland. A child answered.

"Could I speak with your daddy?" I asked.

"Mr. McAntee," she corrected me gravely.

"Yes," I agreed. "Mr. McAntee."

"Hold on, please."

Bruce's voice sounded like a Wheaties commercial, and I could almost see him holding down his cowlick as we exchanged preliminary pleasantries like our troubles with Miami customs.

I said, "Yeah, they must think everyone's running drugs." Bruce said cryptically that maybe that wasn't far off the mark. I told him I wanted to see him and he suggested lunch the next day at Horse Feathers in Portland. I agreed.

When I hung up, my friend said, "You must have met Tony Hendryks."

"What makes you say that?" I asked.

She shrugged. "The Panama connection, and you know me: two plus two and I get six."

On my way back to the party I mulled over the answer I had gotten when I added up my own column of twos.

Maria's interest in the disappearance of Carlos Pardo, aka Chester Brown, and her exchange of Tony's surname for his aunt Georgie's: Brown for Hendryks. Those two twos plus another: Maria had introduced Tony as her cousin, and I remembered Bruce McAntee, on the porch of Georgie's house in

El Valle, saying, "Carlos Pardo had a sister. Name of Maria."

I got six out of adding all that up. Two plus two plus two. Wouldn't you?

Chapter 4

After dropping Pat off at the convent, I headed
south on Route One, hitting Moody's Diner there in
Waldoboro a little after 11:00 p.m. Of course I
stopped for pie.

They had a vacancy in their tourist cabins, so I
decided to stay the night. Linoleum on the floor, a
little gas heater set in the wall, slatted metal
springs under what felt like a horse-hair mattress.
Olden days.

In Portland, I drove around the old port area

34

fifteen minutes looking for a place to park. Gave up finally and stowed the car in the bowels of a municipal garage.

The decor of Horse Feathers was California International: Boston fern and 'Twenties posters. Bruce, tall and blond and dressed by L.L. Bean, fit right in.

I was dressed in flea market specials — well-laundered jeans, and a turtleneck with a real nice collar still, and a flannel shirt that hid where the seams of the turtleneck had come undone. My sweater hid the three-corner tear in my flannel shirt; but after I took my jacket off, there was nothing to hide my elbows poking shyly through the sweater. I tried to keep my elbows off the table. And I wished we had agreed to meet at McDonald's.

I couldn't tell whether Bruce kept his eyes off my elbows or whether he hadn't noticed them. He seemed glad to see me. He asked about Mother and my cousin Susan. Asked, finally, what was up. Good question.

After a not-so-hot night's sleep, waking to the bright clarity of a cold October morning, I hadn't been sure just why I had called him. Brushing my teeth, contemplating my reflection in the mottled mirror at Moody's, I suspected that my call to Bruce had had something to do with my antagonism toward Alex. Just what that consisted of, I didn't force myself to figure out. But I did notice how comfortable I felt whenever I imagined explaining to my dinner companions of the evening before that Clara had had nothing to do with Chester Brown's disappearance. And how good it seemed when I pictured myself exposing some unspecified crime committed by Barney and by Alex, contrasting their wrong-doing to Clara's innocence.

I told Bruce, "I think I met Chester Brown's sister. You said he had a sister named Maria. Maybe your age? Red hair?"

Bruce nodded. "Sounds like her."

"Her name's Papandreou," I said. "Now."

"Yeah," Bruce agreed. "She's had a few husbands."

That surprised me. Most dykes I know have been married. Some still are. But usually, once is enough. I said, "Oh yeah?"

"Last one was a Greek. Obviously."

"But she doesn't live with him," I probed.

"No. Lives with a woman. Alex Adler. She's more your age. They've been together quite a while. Off and on," he amended.

He said it matter-of-factly, surprising me again. Homosexual liaisons are, my family and all their friends seem to think, catastrophes.

I said, "Oh."

We ate a while in silence.

"I thought you weren't interested," said Bruce.

I said, "I'm not."

"Too bad." He said, "You want dessert?"

I did.

"We could really use you," he said, after giving our order: two strawberry cheesecakes.

"Use me? What do you mean, use me?"

"Come back," he said, "to my office. We'll talk about it there."

His office was in the same building as Horse Feathers, upstairs and down a long corridor with many doors into other offices. I read the names, most of them uninformative: One Up, Hair Today, Women Unlimited. The sign on the door Bruce brought us to read *Stars and Stripes*.

"*Stars and Stripes?*" I said.

He laughed, stepping aside to usher me in. "Carlos," he said. "Or Chester."

The office was small, about ten by twelve. Opposite the door a grimy window looked out onto the fire escapes of other office blocks. A battered metal desk in front of the window held a computer, monitor and printer. Bookshelves, messy with papers and open boxes of junk, ran along one wall. The other wall had been painted blue, dark blue, and smack in the center of it, hanging crooked, was a photo of Ronald Reagan, the kind you used to see in Post Offices.

"Where's Bush?" I asked.

Bruce dismissed Ronnie with a wave of his hand. "Oh, that," he said. And then, "Carlos."

The room was depressing. And dirty. "You hang out here much?" I asked.

"Not at all. Or hardly at all. The office was Carlos's idea. He used that —" Bruce pointed at the computer, "— to put out our newsletter. His newsletter. It's a Macintosh. Desktop publishing. I should sell it. Or give it to someone. You want it?"

I could kill for it. "Sure," I said. "How much?" If it was under ten dollars, I could probably swing it.

"Sit down," he said, stirring the dust on the seat of the only chair. He propped himself on the corner of the desk. "This," he said, "is what it's all about. You ever hear of CENTAC?"

I hadn't and he explained that it was an

experimental unit the Drug Enforcement Agency had developed in Miami. "Two years ago, Carlos approached me to start a CENTAC team here in Maine. I say team — but all it ever was was Carlos and me."

According to Bruce, they had been behind the investigations of several recent notorious cases. "I understand," I said, "that Chester Brown was in Immigration and Naturalization, an INS man."

"That's right," Bruce agreed. "His cover."

"Is Chester Brown Carlos?"

"That's right. The story, what he told me, is he was Dito Brown's bastard. So is Maria. Different mothers. Carlos's mother was Indian. Woman named Bonifacio. I knew her. She used to clean for us."

Bruce began to pull the knuckles, one by one, of his left hand. The thumb was stubborn. It wouldn't pop. "Please," I said.

"Oh, sorry. Drives Mary nuts. My wife." He shoved his hands into his jacket pockets, out of temptation's way, and resumed his story.

Maria's mother had raised both children. In Harlem. Her dowry, a small trust supplied by Dito's family through his sister, Georgie Hendryks, had attracted the protection of an Irish immigrant who married her and provided a home of sorts for the children.

The boy had been christened Charles, a name he hated. When he was thirteen, he discovered that his father wasn't the bum who had raised him, but a misty and romantic figure from South of the Border. He started to call himself Carlos.

"Where did the Chester come in?" I asked.

"He did that in the Navy. Dito's family, the

38

American side, as I'm sure you know, once owned a good chunk of Maryland's Eastern Shore. The family name was Chester. Chestertown? He changed his name to Chester Brown."

"And Pardo? Why Pardo?"

"Pardo is Spanish for Brown. Chester Brown, Carlos Pardo."

"In the papers, they implied he was a drug runner and used the name Carlos Pardo for that."

"Well, he didn't run drugs. And he never used the name Pardo that I know of."

"Never?"

"Well, we teased him sometimes. Called him Carlos Pardo. But, no, he never used it."

"It sounds," I said, "like the person who planted the stories about him in the papers when he disappeared must have known him well."

"Either that or knew Spanish and just made up the Pardo."

"Narrows it down a lot."

I worked on the relationships in silence for a while.

"Carlos, Maria and Tony," I said. "They're siblings. All with the same father."

"That's right."

I asked, "So, what do you call him?"

"Carlos. I call him Carlos. The Chester was official. Carlos was for friends."

"And you're his friend?" My eyes roamed the dark blue wall with Ronnie's crooked picture in the center of it.

Bruce shrugged. "I ran across Carlos in Nam," he explained. "In 'seventy. Looked me up. Said he knew me. Surprised me. I didn't remember him. The summer of 'fifty-nine he stayed with Georgie in El Valle, he said. So, of course I'd met him. But he was younger than me, and I just don't remember. Do you remember him?"

"We left in 'fifty," I said.

Bruce rose and walked behind the desk. He stood gazing out the window. It had begun to rain. Or sleet. Whatever, it pinged sharply on the glass and sounded cold.

"Turned out Georgie kinda kept an eye on the two kids. That one summer she brought both of them to Panama. She and Maria never got along. But Carlos adored her."

Georgie must have cared for him too, for she'd sent him to Stanford. There he joined ROTC. His first tour of duty had taken him to Nam. His request. Carlos, according to Bruce, had always been a super-patriot.

"You know how it is," he said, turning again to face me.

I did know. Many Zonians, and former Zonians, are super-patriotic. For those of us who aren't thrilled about invading Grenada and bombing Khadafy, it can be difficult to separate our emotions from our politics and keep our focus unblurred. Like reading complex road signs after one too many. Difficult and possibly dangerous, as I was to discover.

"I had just retired here to Maine," Bruce continued, once more settling his haunch on the corner of the desk, "when who turns up on my doorstep but Carlos."

Carlos, who had been with the INS since 'seventy-five, was after drug czars and "illegal aliens." "He seemed," Bruce explained, "to regard them as one and the same, even the refugees from El Salvador and Guatemala."

"Why," I asked, "did you agree to help him, then."

Bruce snorted. His derision, apparently, was for himself. "Boredom!" he said. "Retirement isn't what it's cracked up to be. Neither is a White Christmas. All my life I dreamed of retiring to New England. After I had put in my twenty years, Mary and I came to Maine, took over her folks' place in Fryeburg."

"What happened?"

"Nothing happened. Carlos happened. I was bored and Carlos happened. I knew he had his head up his ass, but the drugs were real. And bad. I wanted to help. I even thought, at first, that I could control Carlos . . ." Bruce shook his head. "Forget it. Mary wouldn't have him in the house."

"Why?" I asked.

"She said Carlos made Male Chauvinist Pigs look good."

"He make a pass at her?"

"Good Lord, no. They don't come straighter than Carlos. That's how I know he never dealt drugs. He was incapable of being crooked. No, Mary said he frightened her."

Bruce studied the floor as if the answer to the mystery had been spun into the dust balls lying there. His cowlick had come unsprung and, hands in pockets, he looked about eighteen, the way Van Heflin always used to. It was hard to think of him as retired.

"Mary said he was a bully. Asked her why." He

shrugged. "Said she knew, that's all. Anyway, never having him to the house, it put a strain on the relationship. You know."

"Yeah," I said. Then, "They often go together, super-patriot —" I nodded at Ronnie's picture — "and bully. I think they call it being macho."

"Yeah," said Bruce, not too interested. "Anyway, I took the job with CENTAC. Our cover was this monthly newsletter, *Stars and Stripes*. We fingered maybe a dozen people, kept some drugs off the street. Kept them on their toes at least. Then Carlos gets this obsession about illegal aliens."

"Refugees," I said.

"Yeah," said Bruce. "What I kept telling him: Refugees."

Carlos's prejudice had started when evidence surfaced that drugs had begun to flow into the States from Canada. Working as he did with the INS, Carlos knew that refugees from Central America had begun to pour across the border at St. Stephen's, the New Brunswick point of entry.

"Asshole couldn't count," Bruce said. "He figured the Central Americans — and the North Americans helping them — they were just a narco gang. The church support, the media support — the media support, that really made him loco — he thought it was all camouflage. You know, like *The Purloined Letter*. He used to say, 'Where do you hide illegal crossings better than with other illegal crossings?'" Bruce cocked a finger at me. "It made a crazy kind of sense."

"You mean," I asked, incredulous, "you bought that?"

"For Christ's sake! No. I told you, he had his head up his ass."

But Bruce had been unable to restrain his partner. Carlos became increasingly obsessed with the refugee flow through Monte Cassino. Despite Bruce's refusal to participate, Carlos had planned a raid on the island in December, 1987.

"Then this Northeaster blew up and they had to call off the raid. But that's the last anyone ever heard of Carlos. Evidently he refused to leave when the rest did. They all assumed he went on out to the island. You see, Monte Cassino is like an island —"

I cut him off. "I know," I said, "I've been there."

"Well, that's the last place Carlos was known to be."

"The Immaculate Conception," I murmured.

"Pardon me?" After a moment, Bruce said, "If he is alive, one person who'd know is Georgie. Carlos would be sure to get in touch with her."

"Well, someone should talk to Georgie."

"That," said Bruce, "is where you come in."

Chapter 5

And that's how I found myself at Tocumen Airport in Panama City three weeks to the day after I had left there in September. But back then my pockets had been empty. Now I had a thousand dollars in traveler's checks, plus a new credit card. For expenses.

"Sky's the limit," Bruce had said. "Just find out what happened to Carlos."

An official investigation, he told me, had gotten them nowhere. "I read your last book," he said. "And

I just thought you might be able to ferret out some more information. Where you know Georgie."

I had reminded him that he knew Georgie too.

"That was the trouble, I think. She knew, or suspected, I was with the government."

Bruce also gave me a retainer. Another thousand. With it, I paid some bills including rent that was overdue.

I had decided to spend my last night in the convent with Pat. She had agreed to take me to the airport in the morning. My flight left at 7:35 a.m. That last afternoon I spent running around. In Blue Hill, I stopped at Robert Jardin's pharmacy to pick up some toothpaste for the trip. The young man in charge said Mr. Jardin was in his office. I said I wouldn't bother him, but just then Robert appeared through the door at the back. He was bent and dusty looking and I might not have recognized him but for the manager's smile, which was one made for bosses. Robert's face, partially hidden by a green eye-shade, looked pinched, though he brightened some when he saw me. His eyes, deep in their sockets, reminded me of someone, Bela Lugosi, maybe. He made me nervous and I started to babble about buying toothpaste for my trip to Panama.

Robert said he envied me and asked whether I thought I would see Georgie this time. When I said I hoped to, he said to say hello to her for him. He even inquired about Mother.

On my way back to Pat's convent, I stopped in at H.O.P.E. to say some good-byes. My friend Edith told me to give Noriega a Bronx cheer if I ran into him. I didn't promise. I stopped at Maria's, but only Alex was there, so I didn't stay. The tides were wrong, so I couldn't very easily get out to Monte Cassino to see Clara, even if I had wanted to. I did want to, but since I was spending the night with Pat, I thought better of it.

Barney was home that night, so conversation at the convent jerked along like a Model T low on gas. After we went to bed, though, Pat sighed in my ear a lot, again, and that made up for everything.

The next day, on the way to Bangor, I told her a little about my trip, but not much. I didn't want to get into a fight. I just said I had a lead on Chester Brown and that a friend of the family was paying for my flight. She didn't ask any questions.

I said, "I wish you were coming with me."

She said, "The last time I went with you somewhere, you almost got us killed."

That was an exaggeration. What really happened to upset her was that the New York Police now have a file on her, and somewhere in that file is the suggestion that she and I were lovers. A fate, apparently, if not worse than death, equivalent to it. I let it pass.

I landed in Tocumen just before 8:00 p.m. It was warm and humid, the smell of ozone sharp in the air after a cloudburst. It was rainy season I remembered, and I had forgotten to bring a raincoat.

It happened as I stood in line waiting to rent myself a car. It wasn't until I felt her hand on my elbow that her question registered.

"Señora, señora. Is it you?"

I didn't recognize her. She wasn't quite my height, and when I had seen her last, she was half a head taller. She was mestiza, Indian and European, and beautiful. Her aquiline nose suggested Spain, or at least the Mediterranean. Her mouth was wide, her lips full still, although she seemed to be my age, some gray showing through the black hair pulled severely from her face and knotted at the nape of her neck, exposing the broad high cheekbones, the dark brows and almond eyes.

"Bonifacio," she said.

Of course. I remembered. I had been about twelve when Bonifacio came to iron for us. Just once a week, and only for a couple of months. To help out Clemmie, our Jamaican maid. Clementine, Mother had said, needed a rest. Bonifacio, Mother had added, needed a job. Mother had once confided in me: Bonifacio had gotten herself in trouble. Getting in trouble meant getting a baby without having a marriage certificate to hang over your bed. That was just a figure of speech: Mother kept a crucifix over hers, and, as I was to find out, so did Bonifacio.

All this and more rattled through my mind as I stood in the Avis line at Tocumen Airport staring at her. The more had to do with Bruce's telling me that the Bonifacio who was Carlos's mother had once worked for his family. My adult mind rearranged childhood information.

"Bonifacio?" I echoed her.

She nodded, laughing. "Bonifacio."

"How did you know me?"

The dazzling teeth I remembered were mostly gone, but her easy mouth, now as then, was familiar with humor. She scrabbled excitedly in her purse, and pulled out an envelope with U.S. postage. She selected one photo from several and held it out to me.

There I was, standing with Maria, Maria holding a chainsaw, me loppers. It was a Polaroid snapshot taken by a volunteer at Monte Cassino just the weekend before.

"Maria," said Bonifacio, pointing. Then, triumphantly, "You!"

"Where on earth did you get this?"

She looked up into my eyes, surprised by the question. "Carlos."

"Carlos sent you this?"

"Yes. Carlos. My son."

Bonifacio seemed as eager as I to continue our reacquaintance, and she waited while I completed the paperwork to rent the car. She invited me to visit.

Bonifacio had a room on a side street of San Miguelito, a brassy new district on the way into Panama City. San Miguelito is as poor as Chorillo, the older part of Panama down by the Presidential Palace and the National Cathedral, but it's different — upbeat, lively. Too lively. I drove slow. If I hit someone, the damage would be slight. My caution amused Bonifacio. But then, life seemed to amuse her. Several times she called a greeting to someone. Once she reached out and took hold of a young boy who ran alongside the car speaking rapidly to her in Spanish. "My grandson," she explained.

Bonifacio's side street was dark, as was her stairwell. But she had a pencil flashlight in her bag to light the way. Her room was on the third floor in back. The building, though concrete and fairly new, smelled of garbage and urine, smelled of poverty.

If Bonifacio lived alone, she was keeping someone's clothes for him; pants and shirts, dresses and blouses hung neatly on hangers from nails in the wall. A double bed filled half the room. The only other furniture, aside from a battered enamel sink and cupboard unit, was a drop-leaf table by the door and two metal folding chairs. A naked bulb hung from the center of the ceiling.

She gestured me to sit down. From a cardboard box she kept under the bed Bonifacio extracted two mugs and a saucepan. She heated water on an electric hot plate for instant coffee. She served mine generously sweetened with sugar and condensed milk. I managed to sip it without gagging.

She returned to the foot of the bed and knelt, I thought for a crazy moment to pray: a heavy bronze crucifix hung on the wall above. But she was after something in a battered suitcase stowed there. She brought the photograph album and laid it reverently in my hands.

All the photographs were of Carlos. From infancy, through Stanford and Nam. I watched him age, page by page. The last few pictures had been taken recently — taken since Carlos had disappeared. In labored lettering the place and date of each photo was marked on a slip of paper. The last few, like the one she had shown me at Tocumen, had been taken in Manhattan, mostly in Harlem. Bonifacio beamed as she helped me turn the pages, explaining some of the events, like graduations, with great pride.

When I had finished admiring the photos, and the album had been replaced in the suitcase beneath the bed, Bonifacio's attention began to wander. It occurred to me the owner of the pants was waiting for her somewhere. But I had questions I wanted answered.

"Carlos, he is a good son to you?"

She drew her fine dark eyes reluctantly from the window. "Yes?" she said.

"Carlos, he is good to you? A good son?"

"Oh, sí, sí. Carlos is my son." Her smile had had much practice at reassuring. "A good son."

"He writes often?"

"Sí, sí. Often."

"Do you see him much?"

She looked puzzled. She said, "He send many pictures."

"Yes," I admitted, "many pictures. But not money?" I probed.

She brightened. "Money, sí. Money."

She rose from the table and knelt again at the foot of the bed. This time she extracted a zippered leather pouch which she gave to me with the same air of reverence as she had placed the photo album in my hands.

The pouch contained gold chains. Her slender fingers stirred the supple metal. A glittering pool of it slipped and flowed from her hand, cascading into the dark well of the pouch.

"From Carlos?" I asked, surprised. Even fenced, the contents of the bag would have purchased a decent apartment.

The pool of metal shining in her hand seemed to

have mesmerized her. Bonifacio, blissful, whispered, "Carlos."

It was way past my bedtime, and my brain felt muddled. I thought, *I guess I can go home; Carlos is alive and well somewhere in Harlem.* I asked Bonifacio for a photo to use as proof. She removed one from its plastic sheath. The caption was dated July 6 89. It showed Carlos smiling under a street sign. Adam Clayton Powell Jr. Blvd., it read.

"He lives there?" I asked.

"Yes. New York City."

"Wouldn't you like to visit him?"

Her blank look suggested it was time for me to go. I asked for his address.

"I don't have," she said.

"How do you write to him?"

That amused her. "Write!" she said and she laughed. She pointed at herself and shook her head, laughing. She pressed the picture into my hands. She seemed to want to get rid of us both.

Something about it didn't compute. Later, approaching Albrook on my way to Curundu where I would be staying, I caught the sheen of moonlight on water where the Pacific tamely approaches the Miraflores locks. "The land divided, the world united." Simple effects requiring elaborate constructions. Later, I thought, I'll think about it later.

When I reached Curundu and my cousin Susan's house, I found her watching a tape of Mancuso. She seemed sleepy. Running marathons in ninety degree heat and a hundred percent humidity would tire me, too, I thought.

"No, I didn't run today," she told me. "But do you know what time it is?"

Only then did I realize how late it had gotten — a little after midnight. I apologized. "We'll go right to bed," I suggested.

"Oh no we won't!" said Susan. "I want to know what you're doing here. And how long you can stay."

She brewed some tea and we gossiped a while. Of my many cousins, Susan always has seemed to have the most energy. Her hair is the reddest, she has the most freckles, and, of course, she's the most athletic. While we sat and talked and laid some plans, she absent-mindedly braided her hair into a long rope that hung down the center of her back. To me that was like knitting in the movies.

Before we went to bed I asked would she like to go with me to El Valle. It seemed, having come so far, silly not to see Georgie, even if I no longer had to regarding Carlos.

Silly not to see her, perhaps. But the thought of meeting her again was scary. So long as Georgie was young and glamorous, I too, was young. And I could be glamorous, too, someday. When I grew up.

What happens, I wondered, when the golden image of infinite glamour turns to the dross of impending death?

Susan had to work, so I drove to El Valle alone. All the way there I imagined Georgie Hendryks. I imagined her in every place I had ever seen her and in some where I never had. Like her bedroom and her bed. Like in the shower. Like across the breakfast table.

The Dutchman's, where I used to go for eggs that summer I'd fallen in love, was a ruin, the watercress beds returned to jungle, the chicken house bent with age. Where I used to lie and watch for Georgie, someone had built a summer cottage. At Georgie's, the gate was open and I drove in.

A woman about my age, her hair gray and cropped, rather like mine, opened the door. She wore jodhpurs and short jodhpur boots. She smelled agreeably of horse, and, slightly, of perfume. Joy Parfum.

"Yes?" she said.

"I'm looking for Georgie Hendryks."

"You've found her," the woman said.

I said, "I'll be damned."

"Oh, I hope not. Have we met?"

When I told her that we had and when, she chuckled, a warm sound from deep in her throat. She said, "Not Brigid. Not the little girl who kept this house under surveillance one summer. The summer the Korean War broke out I think. We wondered, spying on us, whether you imagined us as being Russians or Chinese. You've probably forgotten all about it."

I said, "Yeah."

"Come in, come in. What brings you to the Valley?"

I declined the rum and coke she offered me, settling instead for a glass of orange juice which she squeezed as I stood awkwardly by and watched.

We sat on the veranda in back, where Bruce and

I had sat just a few weeks before. I told her about that visit. She said she was sorry she had missed us. She asked about Mother, and about Susan. I told her I had seen her nephew Tony, Dito's son, only a few days before in Maine. But she wasn't interested in Tony. Or maybe she would just rather have forgotten him. Him and his dreadful giggle.

"I was about to go riding," she said. "Would you like to join me?"

It had been years since I had ridden, and then only Western. Georgie, I remembered, rode English. Once, I had seen her ride side-saddle. She'd worn a long dress and a little round hat.

I said, "Er."

She said, "I see. Can I quote you? You used to have a beautiful saddle," she said, "from Penenome I think you told me. I have a Western saddle, not as pretty as that one, but it should do. Has it been a while? I have a very gentle mare. You shouldn't have any trouble."

I managed not to disgrace myself. As we approached the hotel, Georgie said, "Shall we ride up to the spring where the gold frogs are? My brother Dito and I one summer went there every morning."

Probably the summer of my stake-out, for I had met the two of them there once. It was very early, and in the pale wash of jungle light they looked to me like two movie stars. When I got home that evening it was all I could talk about. Mother told my father later, after I had gone to bed and she believed I was asleep, "I think our little girl's in love." She was right. I was. But Mother had been thinking of Dito and his elastic biceps, not Georgie with her intoxicating breasts.

"Yeah," I said engagingly to Georgie. "Let's."

"Do you remember that summer we met up there at the spring? I was with Dito. The three of us rode together?"

"Yeah," I said, my heart doing funny things in my chest. "I remember. We rode around to the falls."

"Too bad it's so late. We could do that again. The trail's better now. Maybe tomorrow."

I was amazed that she, too, remembered that meeting, that ride. "Maybe tomorrow?" Was she suggesting that I stay the night? Longing disabled my larynx and I couldn't ask.

At the spring we dismounted. Georgie took my hand. "Come," she said. "The frogs have moved. Tourists keep taking them. I thought there weren't any more."

We walked into the jungle, side-by-side, hand-in-hand, wading in the shallow stream.

Where we stopped, a pool had formed. Sunlight, thin, green and watery, filtered through an ocean of leaves, bathed us. Leaves high overhead, turning and shaking in the wind, let the light cascade down in intermittent showers, immersing us in gold and amber, losing us in shadow. Georgie let go of my hand and said, "Sit here. I'll give you a present."

She stood at the back of the pool, motionless. She said, "It takes a while for your eyes to adjust."

I could remember. The frogs were gold, like the light, and they had small black spots, like the shadow. Until your eyes grew accustomed, they blended into their surroundings, invisible. Unless one of them moved. But they too would freeze, as motionless as Georgie. As motionless as I. I remembered. When Georgie and Dito came upon me that distant summer day, I had just caught a frog. I had caught it for her and then, as if the wishing in my mind had conjured her, there she had been, high on her white horse, smiling.

Georgie broke into my reverie saying, "Here's a present. I owe you one. You probably don't remember." She handed me a golden frog, descendant I was sure, of the one I had once given her.

There is no lingering dusk in Panama, and in the Valley evening comes early, when the sun dips behind the mountain rim. We ate by candlelight on a screened-in porch. Georgie had wine, and when we finished with our salad, she offered me brandy. I managed to turn it down. It was cool, so we moved indoors.

Chinese rugs, sapphire and cream, acres of them, like islands, lay on the polished tile floor; and bamboo furniture, reminding me of my childhood, floated like moored junks in intimate clusters here and there in the dimly lit room, the ceiling high as the sky and lost in shadow.

Georgie gestured me to a sofa facing a wide expanse of glass. I sat. She turned off the lights. In a moment my eyes had adjusted to the dark and the Milky Way blazed bright. It seemed, as I relaxed, my head thrown back against the cushion, as if the stars were in the Valley, not the sky, close by, not far away at all.

Georgie sat next to me. Close by. Her leg touched

mine. Her thigh from hip to knee pressed mine. My throat felt dry, my palms wet.

I said, "Good view."

She said nothing.

I said, "You ever hear from Carlos?"

She said, "Carlos," and her finger touched my ear, the rim of my ear, lightly. She let it run down to the lobe, then feather-light, her fingers brushed my cheek before drifting away and touching, for just a moment, my ear again.

The moisture between my legs came in a hot and sudden ejaculation. I must have moaned. She said, "Are you all right?"

I said, "Yeah. I'm all right."

Her hand lay on the inside of my thigh that was pressed next to hers. The same light finger began to caress the seam of my crotch.

She said, "You're wet."

She said it in my ear, the warm tip of her tongue touching the hollow of my ear. Her hand left my crotch, busied itself with my belt, with my zipper, and came home free. The orgasm, like flood waters bursting from a dam, pulsed through me, leaving me, finally, weak and helpless.

She said, "Poor kitten was hungry. Shall we go to bed?"

Chapter 6

I woke slowly. I had slept deeply. Unfamiliar odors and unfamiliar sounds brought me gently to consciousness. Cunt and coral vine smell good together I thought drowsily, placing the scents. In the distance, Billie Holliday sang about love. I thought about it.

First thought: It's like riding a bicycle.

I chuckled into my pillow, which smelled divine: Joy Parfum and cunt mingled there.

The coral vine, susurrant in the breeze, climbed

outside the window, its tendrils twisted in the iron stems and flowers of the grille above my head.

You don't forget how, I said to myself. For me, it had been so long I'd wondered.

But then, it wouldn't have mattered. Not with Georgie. With Georgie I would have learned instantly. Remembered instantly.

The air was cool, it must still be morning I thought. I burrowed more deeply under the covers, sliding my pillow, redolent with sex, down with me. Billie Holliday and the coral vine receded as the odors and sounds of the night enveloped me. I wondered where Georgie was and I hoped she would soon return.

For a while, drifting in and out of sleep, I comforted myself while I waited, waited for her to come and take over. Now and then, I heard Billie complain about a lover who was slow. I sympathized.

And then the terrible moment arrived when I couldn't wait any longer. I threw back the covers and opened my eyes to a glorious day.

On the oriental brass and mahogany bedside table stood a bouquet of cut flowers. An envelope marked "Kitten" leaned against the crystal vase. A Chinese silk robe lay folded on a bamboo footrest; embroidered silk scuffs waited demurely to one side. I shrugged myself into the robe and, tying it around me, walked barefoot to the john.

I had seen myself look worse after an all-night bout of lovemaking. But then, I hadn't had one since I stopped drinking. That was a few twenty-four hours ago. I wondered how Georgie had looked that morning. And I wondered when she had gotten up. I wondered, finally, and briefly, how I could have carried that Grace Kelly albatross around my neck all these years, avoiding life while I mooned over glamour. I only knew how light I felt for having shed it. Relieved, I sauntered back to the bedroom, to my cut flowers, to my *billet doux.*

The note paper was expensive vellum, cream-colored, with an embossed monogram, *G H,* elaborately scrolled across the front. Inside it said, "Kitten, good morning. And thank you. I am off to Cartagena. Awfully glad I didn't miss you this time. Georgie."

Thank you?

Glad I didn't miss you?

My rage, which I also thought I had lost in the interstices of sobriety and age, flashed bright as memory. In its brilliance, Georgie's crystal vase with its burden of flowers became history. Then I took a step and cut my foot on a piece of glass. That calmed me down. But I was glad to see my blood mar the perfect cream of her Persian carpet. She'd never get it out, I thought, if I set the stain with some boiling water. But first I took off her creepy robe, found my trousers and slipped into them. They smelled disgusting.

In the kitchen, where I, bashful as a twelve-year-old, had so recently watched Georgie squeezing orange juice for me, coffee waited in a Mr. Coffee brewer. A silver tray beside it contained a cup, silver sugar and creamer, and a croissant wrapped in a linen napkin. While I waited for water to come to a boil, I ate the croissant and drank some coffee. I didn't take much of the boiling water back to the bedroom with me; I didn't think it would take much to set the stain.

My foot had stopped bleeding. I had found a Band-Aid in the medicine chest. Back in the bedroom I decided to finish dressing before I set the stain. I put on my shoes and socks. Then I combed my hair. By that time, I decided the water wasn't hot enough any longer, so I went back to the kitchen to boil some more.

While I waited, I had another cup of coffee. On a shelf above the kitchen table I noticed a photograph album. Idly, I pulled it down and opened it. The first few pages were of Georgie when she was young — as she was when I first fell in love with her. Georgie and other girls, other women. Some I had known, and one looked familiar, though I wasn't sure why. Disgusted, I shut it, slamming the back cover over it. But as I did so, I noticed a picture of Maria. I opened the album again and saw several pages with missing pictures. I could tell they were missing because they had been mounted long ago with those glue-on corners they used back then. The missing pictures were all of Carlos. I could tell by the captions, written in Georgie's bold hand. Bold and flashy. Most unlike the handwriting in Bonifacio's album. The hand was different, but the captions were the same. Word for word the same.

I put the album back and returned to the bedroom. Without the boiling water. I decided my tattered ego would not be mended by destroying a beautiful carpet. I gathered my things and started to leave. At the door I turned back. It took me fifteen minutes to get the blood out of Georgie's rug. Then I checked everywhere for anything I might have left behind. Superstition. To be sure I'd never return. The thought of coming back made me shudder. Never mind I'd spent nearly half a century longing to be there.

At the Y where the road enters the valley floor, I turned up toward the hotel. There I ordered lunch and ate it on the veranda, looking out toward the Sleeping Princess where, before the summer I fell in love, I would go on expeditions with my horse, Caramelo. Where I had discovered, one hot and cloudless day, the Pacific Ocean, and realized in doing so that only men, white men, did memorable things, things that got written into history books.

I steadfastly did not look the other way where Georgie's house was visible, and the place where all one summer I had lain in the grass, in the ticks, training my binoculars on the most beautiful woman in the world.

The road leaving the valley peaked on the mountain rim and then the foothills fell gently to the coastal plain where the wide Pacific stretched across the whole horizon. Ochre grasses sprang from the red volcanic soil, and the ocean, where they met, was brutally blue. That day, above it all, gently touching everything, the sky hovered, pale blue and white.

When amazement of the beauty, and terror of the twisting road, subsided, I felt somewhat restored. My raveled ego mending, I thought about what I should do next. I had planned to leave, tail between my legs, on the first flight home. But now I decided that before I left I would drive to San Miguelito and see Bonifacio again.

I wasn't aware of the truck behind me until it tried to pass. But there was no way anyone could pass on that stretch of road. A sheer drop on my side, and on the other boulders and rock slides made even the oncoming traffic dangerous. I honked and gestured out my window for the driver to stay back. Through my rear view mirror, I could see that he was young and Indian, with hair longer than the young men in the valley wear theirs.

He threw me a bird and started to pass again. This time he hit my rear fender.

I had been going slow, about twenty-five miles an hour. But as I lost control of the car, my brain seemed to slide into low gear, as if my body knew this moment was its last and meant to savor it. The road dropped out of sight and all I could see before me was an endless blue sky with soft white clouds, and there, in the middle distance, a big black bird soared, a vulture it was, with wing-spread wide and graceful as any a seagull's on the coast of Maine. I wondered if he had a name, and I hoped that it wasn't Jonathan. I hate the name Jonathan. In my new existence inside the vulture I didn't want to be a Jonathan. Not even part of a Jonathan.

I believe I passed out for only an instant. I don't remember hitting the tree. Opening my eyes, I saw it was the only tree in sight, lonely, but sturdy, with branches reaching up to the road. When I got over the shakes, I climbed out of the car, onto a branch and made my way up it. A crowd had gathered. When I appeared, they began to clap.

They were happy. But you could tell that Jonathan wasn't. Despondent, he dipped low on the other side of my car.

You can't keep everyone happy all the time, I thought, and giggled. An elderly woman with a blanket in her hands approached me. She wrapped the blanket around my shoulders and urged me to sit. I didn't argue. My knees had turned to jelly. I felt the softness of her flesh as my body slid alongside hers to the ground.

The accident happened a little after one in the afternoon. By four o'clock, Susan was there, emitting energy like a dynamo. Energy enough, fortunately, for both of us.

The car had been winched up and towed away, and a policeman had questioned witnesses. Witnesses, but not me. My friend with the blanket wouldn't let him. I think he may have been her grandson, the way she brushed him out of the house she had brought me to, a one-room adobe hut with a thatched roof. I learned that her name was Blanca, and that she was very kind. She fed me sweet coffee, and then some chicken broth. I must have slept awhile. It seemed one minute I was sipping broth and the next Susan was hugging me.

We didn't hit La Boca, where the Canal begins, until after dark. Frank, Susan's mild-mannered husband, had supper ready and warm for us. By the time I'd finished a bowl of Cherry Garcia for dessert,

I felt quite restored. Ready to visit Bonifacio. I asked whether I could borrow their car.

"No way!" sparked Susan. She stood facing me, arms across her chest like a defensive tackle, her braids, bright and brassy, wound about her head like a helmet.

Nettled, I said I'd take a taxi then.

She wouldn't hear of that either. "I'll take you," she said. "That way, no one'll have to get me out of bed to come rescue you."

She said it with a laugh. I decided she really wanted to come. Frank, though, didn't seem happy about her taking off to San Miguelito at ten o'clock at night. But his protests were half-hearted, as though experience had taught him they were useless.

In the car, Susan asked, "What's up, anyhow?"

I said, "What do you mean, what's up?"

She said, "Don't play games. The fellow who called me, he's a schoolteacher, he said someone deliberately ran you off the road up there in El Valle."

I hadn't thought about it. That afternoon I had gone from shock to euphoria. But looking back, I remembered the driver of the truck, his youth, his long hair. I said, "Naw. He was on drugs."

"Well," said Susan. "Whatever, the guy who called me said it was deliberate. Why this trip to San Miguelito? And why tonight?"

I said, "Did you know Carlos Brown? He's Georgie Hendryk's nephew. She brought him down to El Valle one summer when you all were in high school."

Susan couldn't remember any Carlos Brown, not back then, not ever.

I said, "Bruce couldn't remember him either. Bruce McAntee. Carlos is supposed to be Dito's illegitimate son."

Susan said he wouldn't be the only one, she supposed.

I told her about Carlos's approach to Bruce and their partnership in CENTAC. I finished by saying that Bruce thought Georgie would know where Carlos was, if Carlos were alive.

"So," said Susan, "where do you come in?"

I told her Bruce had hired me to approach Georgie.

"Why do that?" she asked. "Bruce knows her real well, probably better than you. He used to hang around there a lot when we were kids. Summers."

I said I didn't know. And I didn't. Had never even thought about it until that minute. Thinking about it, I didn't care for the possibilities.

I asked, "Didn't Georgie ever get married?"

Susan laughed. "Not hardly."

I let it go.

She said, "So what did you find out?"

What I had found out, I didn't intend to share. I had found out that Georgie Hendryks was sexually manipulative. I had found out that Brigid Donovan was a push-over. And I had just discovered that Bruce McAntee was an S.O.B. He had known all along that Georgie would take me to bed. He had paid all that money for pillow talk. Served him right there hadn't been any. Or none that would interest anyone but a voyeur.

"Nothing," I said. "I didn't find out anything."

66

"She's in Cartagena," said Susan matter-of-factly. I didn't contradict her, glad not to have to explain I had spent the night with her. Spent the night with her and except for that one idle question never talked about Carlos at all.

"You still haven't told me," Susan said, "why you need to go to San Miguelito."

I told her I had been in Georgie's house and had looked at the photograph album. I told her about the missing pictures and about the photos Bonifacio had shown me. I told her Georgie must have set me up at the airport because the pictures Bonifacio had shown me, in order to convince me that Carlos was alive, had come from Georgie's album. Since I didn't have a clue why Georgie would do that, or how she had known I was coming, I slid over that. And I slid over how I happened to be in Georgie's house, looking through photograph albums, when she was away in Cartagena. But Susan didn't ask. She either didn't care why I had made myself at home, or, worse thought, she knew without asking.

At 10:30 p.m., San Miguelito was jumping. I had a little trouble finding Bonifacio's building. Susan had a little trouble finding a place to park. She was nervous about leaving her car out on the street — an alley really, and dark. A kid offered to watch it for her. He looked like Bonifacio's grandson. I was afraid to ask, afraid that all the urchins on the street that time of night looked alike to me.

Neither Susan nor I had a flashlight. We groped our way up the stairs. The odor was familiar, but that didn't mean much. In all the stairwells of San Miguelito, probably, the same odors brewed. Urine, rancid oil, rotting vegetables.

Where I thought Bonifacio's apartment would be, a crowd of people had gathered. They were somber. More than somber. Pious. The way people look when they hear of tragedy. The mask they wear to protect spontaneous thoughts that form in their heads but which, perhaps, are not acceptable to speak, that must be considered before they are displayed. Later, when the tragedy is older, when it has made a place for itself in their minds, they will laugh. They will laugh for joy at being alive. I knew when I saw them that Bonifacio was dead.

A woman saw me and began to talk excitedly and gesture toward us. The knot of men and women turned as one and looked us over. They seemed less curious than hostile.

I said, *"Buenos noches. Queremos ver a Bonifacio."*

"Gringas! Gringas!" they hissed, the sound like geese in a gaggle, threatening.

The woman who had called attention to our presence began again to chatter. They nodded. Susan took my elbow. She pulled me close.

I said, *"Está aquí? Bonifacio?"*

At that they became silent. A man, young and beautiful, took a step toward us. His blood was mixed, the mixture, common in the Caribbean, of all the people who had ever been to the crossroads of the world, which is to say, of all the people who had ever been: East Indian, West Indian, African, European, Pacific Islanders. Who knows. He said in English, "What do you want?"

"Bonifacio. Yesterday I visited her. We met at the airport."

The troublemaker nodded and chattered. She

68

seemed to be saying, "See. Didn't I tell you." Her audience nodded, and shifted.

"Bonifacio," he said, "is dead."

I had known before he spoke, and I couldn't pretend otherwise.

"You are not surprised," the young man said.

"Yes," I said. "No."

He smiled. But he didn't seem amused. "Yes. No. I don't understand."

"I didn't know. But all of you standing here. I knew something was wrong." I hesitated. "Was it an accident?" I asked.

He had sidled up close to us, his face only inches from mine. Susan, meantime, was pulling me toward the stairwell. I was having trouble holding my ground. Suddenly the young man grabbed my shoulder. "Come," he said. "Look for yourselves."

The body was gone. But not the blood. Blood had sprayed the wall, and the ceiling. Blood lay coagulating on the floor beneath the table at which, the night before, Bonifacio and I had sat and looked at photographs of Carlos. I wondered how you accidentally could cut an artery.

The young man thrust his face into mine. With a savage gesture, he ran his thumb from ear to ear, under his jaw, across his throat. "No!" he said. "Not an accident."

Did he think I had done it?

Susan called from the doorway, peremptory and sane. "Brigid, we should go."

My brain was moving very slowly, the way it did when I had sailed into space that afternoon. No buzzards this time. Unless you wanted to count my lovely young man with the big black eyes and curly long lashes. I wanted to bet him his name wasn't Jonathan. Either.

Blood had spattered the clothes hanging neatly from their nails. Jesus still drooped sadly on his bronze cross above the bed. He seemed to have shut his eyes on the scene. He did that, I had noticed before, when things got rough.

On the table stood a mug of cold coffee, a leathery scum floating on its surface. Next to it lay the leather pouch which had contained a small fortune in gold chains. In the center of the table was a photo album. I reached for it.

Pseudo-Jonathan, quicker than a hawk, gripped my wrist.

"The money is already gone," he said.

Susan, still in the doorway, screamed. "Brigid, for Christ's sake, let's get out of here."

"Stolen?" I asked.

"No," he said bitterly. "She gave it to charity."

"Did you live with her?" I asked.

If we had been lovers, I would have liked how close his face was to mine. I might not even have minded how tightly he held my hand in his. But we weren't, and his breath was sour with beer and tobacco.

He blinked, surprised. "Live with her? She was my mother."

"You are Carlos's brother?"

"Carlos? Who's Carlos?"

"Your brother. Carlos."

With my head I gestured to the photo album. "His pictures are in there."

He cast my hand aside and snatched up the

album. "Where," he asked, thrusting it at me, "is this Carlos? Show me."

I would have sworn the album was the same one Bonifacio and I had looked at the night before. But if it was, someone had exchanged the pages. The ones we had looked at together were gone. These were filled with pictures of other children, other young men, one of them Pseudo-Jonathan, who waited expectantly for my reaction.

"Well?" he breathed on me.

I backed away a step.

"Brigid, please," Susan, behind me, implored.

"I guess I was mistaken," I said. "Sorry."

I had been looking at him intently. Otherwise I would have missed the quick sequence of expressions that crossed his face: relief, anxiety, and then cold anger.

"Get out!" he said and pushed me, deliberate and hard, in the chest. Hard enough to bruise, hard enough to make me stumble. Susan caught me and pulled me through the door.

That's as far as we got, the door. The crowd had grown in size and hostility. It had us trapped. I wondered why they were mad at me, what they thought I had done, how they thought I could have been responsible for what had happened to Bonifacio.

Pseudo-Jonathan saved us. "*Dejen passar las gran putas.*" Let the whores go.

And they did, though they continued to jeer at us, and to shove us as we passed.

I hardly remember getting out on the street. I was preoccupied. The word *puta*, whore, echoed loudly in my head. Echoed from the valley of my past, echoed off that Everest of my racist colonial heritage. I remembered how my father had protested the hiring of Bonifacio to iron for us, the words he had chosen: "You're not hiring that nigger whore!"

By the time we reached the street, I knew at least why they were mad at us. And I knew why they seemed to think that I had had something to do with Bonifacio's death. I had.

Bonifacio hadn't been killed for her gold chains. She had been killed for the photo album. I wondered whether, if I had died in the accident, Bonifacio would still be alive. Or had her fate been determined earlier? When Carlos disappeared. When Carlos was born. When Carlos was conceived. I think I knew the answer. Bonifacio's fate had been in her birth, in her beauty, in the circumstances of the straitened existence which allowed her a choice, while she was young, between servitudes.

The car, when we got there, was unattended, but unharmed. Automatically I reached into my trouser pocket for the keys. I felt a piece of paper. It was a note. In the light of the dashboard I read it.

Go home. NOW. NEVER come back. How do you think it will feel to have a bat sewed up your puta cunt?

I didn't show my note to Susan. She didn't ask to see it. In fact, as I read it, she said irritably, "For God's sake, will you drive!"

Chapter 7

There was no point in staying around in Panama any longer. And Susan didn't urge me to. It might have been my imagination, but I thought her husband Frank seemed cool to me at breakfast.

And it occurred to me that the woman who had identified me as Bonifacio's guest might tell the police. I might be tagged "the last person to have seen the victim alive."

I saw that was absurd. After all, a day must have passed between my visit and her death. The accident in El Valle would give me an alibi. But I didn't want to have to contest the point. Pan Am had a flight that afternoon. To Kennedy. I booked it and Susan drove me to Tocumen. As I passed through San Miguelito, the fact of Bonifacio's death came home to me. Grief and a conviction that I was responsible left me somber.

I told Susan just to drop me, not to wait. She didn't protest. But she did get out and give me a hug. She said, "Brigid, I don't know what you're up to. But don't blame yourself for what happened to Bonifacio."

I said, "Yeah."

I got into Kennedy a little before midnight. I had already been through customs in Miami, so all I had to worry about when I landed was finding a place to spend the night.

Nicaragua had been a hazy blue outline off to our left when I had made up my mind to try to find Carlos before returning to Maine. I'd gone back and forth trying to decide whether he was alive or not.

If he was alive, he must have had a hand in setting me up. If he was alive, he must have arranged for Bonifacio's murder, or at least acquiesced in it. If he was alive, Carlos was a monster. He was a matricide. But was he alive?

Someone had made elaborate arrangements to convince me that he was. But did that automatically mean that he wasn't? No. I didn't think so.

If I had simply gone home and reported that Carlos was alive and well in New York City, would the rest have followed? My accident, Bonifacio's murder? I doubted it.

But I hadn't gone home. I had gone instead to El

Valle, to Georgie Hendryks. That visit, I was sure, had set the rest in motion.

On whose orders? To me it hardly mattered. Even if it had been Carlos who ordered the executions, Georgie was the local person in charge. She had made love to me believing that the next night I would be dead.

And whose idea was it to threaten to sew a bat in my vagina? Could a woman do that? Could Georgie do that?

I told the taxi driver to take me to an address in Harlem.

"Look, lady," he said, "it's late, and I'm tired. Where ya wanna go."

"There," I said, irritable from tiredness. "Right where I told you."

"It's your funeral," he said wearily, pulling down the flag and nosing into the traffic.

The address was the Emmaus Hotel. It's not so much a hotel as a shelter. I had discovered the solution to the mystery of that missing nun and her murdered parents there. Perhaps that's what prompted me to give the taxi driver that address. Besides, if my only clue to Carlos's whereabouts placed him on Adam Clayton Powell Boulevard, why spend the night downtown, even if I could think of a place downtown to stay?

At Emmaus, it took me a while to get past security, but eventually they let me in and I spent the night in the women's dormitory. I washed dishes next morning for my bed and board.

Breakfast is in two shifts at Emmaus. The early shift is for residents and volunteers. Then the doors open to whoever is hungry. The line that morning stretched around the corner. Between stints at washing cups and saucers I circulated the picture of Carlos. Three people said they knew that dude. Two gave me an address in the same vicinity, over by the El, past Amsterdam.

I left my gear at Emmaus and took the bus over. On my way out the door, the woman at the desk said, "Hey, you wanna button?" The button was big, black and yellow, and it said Emmaus. I thanked her and pinned it on. A good move. Like wearing a hall pass in school. People noticing it seemed friendly. Several called me Sister.

My fifth lead brought me to a door on the ninth floor of the project.

The woman who answered my knock was elderly and worn, her gray hair pulled tight into a bun. She peered at me over the chain that held the door. She said nothing, just looked, not hostile so much as resigned.

"Good afternoon," I said. "My name is Brigid Donovan and I'm trying to locate this man." I showed her the snapshot.

The door shut abruptly in my face. But then I heard the rattle of the chain being slipped off. When the door reopened, the woman had started across the room. "Shut the door," she said.

The room was small and immaculate, like her. A spider plant hung in the window which was curtained with sheer panels that filtered and softened the light. The woman gestured for me to sit. I had a choice between a worn recliner upholstered in green plastic, and a metal and plastic kitchen chair. I chose the chair. She perched primly on the edge of the recliner.

Her eyes had lost their sparkle and her hair all hint of red. Nonetheless I could see the similarity to Maria in the delicate structure of her bones and the fine shape of her eyes. She sat, erect and silent, waiting but not expectant. You could see she had schooled herself never to expect anything. Never to expect anything except, possibly, the worst.

"I'm from Maine," I offered. She accepted, but offered nothing in return.

"Umh, Carlos, has been missing," I said, "and, uh, friends of his asked me to try to find out what happened to him."

I got up and gave her the picture. She took it but didn't look at it.

"His mother gave that to me. It was taken this past July. I thought you might be able to tell me where he is."

She responded for the first time. She snorted.

When nothing followed, I said, "Is he staying here with you?"

Her look was infinitely scornful. She said, gesturing around her, "Is he?"

I followed the sweep of her hand and realized that it was a one-room apartment, the ottoman in the corner probably unfolding for a bed. "Do you know where he is?" I asked.

"I do not know," she said, "and I do not care."

"When was the last time you heard from him?"

"When that bitch sent him to Stanford," she said, but without much heat.

"To Stanford! That was a long time ago."

"Tell me about it! That bitch, she broke her word." Her jaw snapped shut as if she had said more than she intended and was not likely to repeat her mistake.

"You haven't seen him since he was eighteen?" I asked.

She made no reply. But I could see a spark in her eye. I was determined to nurse that spark into a flame of resentment hot enough to burn down her resistance.

"I thought Georgie Hendryks sent Carlos to Stanford."

At the mention of Georgie's name, the spark flared.

"Was I wrong?"

She couldn't help giving an angry little nod.

"How could you call Georgie a bitch?" I asked. "She's so wonderful! I've known her all my life."

The spark turned to flame. The heat scorched her cheeks, but still she held her tongue.

"Georgie is the most generous person I've ever known," I blew on the spark.

Her grip was slipping, but she kept hold of her silence. Finally I said, blowing a little harder, "Georgie is loyal and she's true to her word."

"She is *not!* She is a *bitch!* And she does *not* keep her word."

The pot boiled over until it was empty. It took Sive Horgan, for that was her name, about ten minutes to tell it all.

In 1947, Sive's sister, Kathleen, arrived on her doorstep with two babies, Carlos and Maria. Maria, a little redhead, was Kathleen's own. Carlos was not.

But they had the same father, one Dito Brown, a young son of the well-to-do family Kathleen had worked for in Panama. Kathleen herself wasn't quite twenty, and she had no intention of caring for these two misbegotten infants, even though she had with her a bank draft for ten thousand dollars, payment to her for agreeing to do just that.

"Ten thousand dollars," Sive leaned forward earnestly to inform me, "wasn't what it is today. Back then, it was a fortune. Of course I said I'd do it. Truth is, I felt sorry for the tykes. Their father was no good, and I knew my sister wasn't no good either. Drank."

So Sive had quit her job at Woolworth's to become a full-time Mom. When word got back to Cork, a friend of the family, Johnny Horgan, sweet-talked her into sending him passage.

"Second biggest mistake of my life," she said sourly. "Drank like a fish. Couldn't keep a job. Pretty soon I was back working at Woolworth's, that ten thousand dollars gone right down the drain."

So she had written to Panama for help. Ten days later Georgie Hendryks appeared at the door.

"The babies then were four. Cute as buttons. Maria especially, pretty as a picture. But Georgie only had eyes for Carlos. Always was that way. Anyway, you could tell she was annoyed at how Kathleen had tricked her like. But she set up this trust is what she called it, and I was to get a check every month. That was either 'fifty or 'fifty-one, I don't remember, but what I got, this was back a ways remember, was three hundred dollars. She said she wanted me to quit my job and get a better place to live. She said to get rid of that bum Horgan, too, but that was easier said than done."

Periodically, the monthly check was increased. When the children were thirteen, Georgie sent tickets and they spent the summer with her in Panama. "Carlos, he loved it. But Maria, she hated Panama and she hated Georgie. Jealous."

After the trip to Panama, Carlos had begun to lord it over Maria, and, when he got big enough, to even knock her around. When Maria quit school at age sixteen, Sive found out that the trust was in the children's name: she lost half her income.

"I had to make do, but that bitch, she sent Carlos a check every month, and if you think he gave me any of it, you have another think coming."

"Did Maria get a check after she left?" I asked.

"Damn right she did. From that trust. Why I only got half as much as before. That bitch started sending Carlos an extra check. To make it up to *him*. Not me! Who had the bills to pay same as ever on half as much money.

At eighteen, Carlos had gone off to Stanford, and that was the last Sive had heard from him.

"You ever hear from Maria?"

"Not for twenty years I didn't hear nothing from her. Then lo and behold about ten months ago I get this letter and it's from her and she wants to know can I tell her where to get hold of Carlos."

Her smile was triumphant: a connoisseur of folly, she had found in Maria's letter the quintessential folly.

"Did you answer it?" I asked foolishly.

She puckered her lower lip disdainfully, answer enough to my question. Of course she hadn't answered Maria's letter.

I tried one more question. "Carlos was here in Harlem just last July. You didn't see him then? He didn't come by?"

"If he *was* here in July, I didn't see him. He never came here to see me. Never. But he used to be in Harlem sometimes. I seen him. What makes you think that picture was taken this year? Last time I saw Carlos was maybe a year and a half ago down there coming off the El, rush hour and he didn't notice me, probably wouldn't't've recognized me even if he did. He had a crew cut. Most always had a crew cut. Only time I ever saw him with hair long like this was way back, five-six years ago, pretending to be a hippie or something God knows what but Johnny Horgan said he was a narc. Settin' up his old pals, Johnny said."

Sive had lost track of her sister, Kathleen, too. "Last I heard of Kathleen musta been ten years already I got a card from Maine, Portland, Maine."

"Did you answer it?"

She looked scornful again. "What would the use of that be?"

I said, "She's your sister."

"Yeah," she said, making it sound like a jeer. "If you see her, let her know."

"You wouldn't have the address," I said.

Triumph replaced scorn. "Of course I have her address, she's my sister ain't she."

It was an address on Congress Street. I thanked

her. At the door she said, "I did write, a helluva lotta good it did me too, but if you see Kathleen tell her . . . Oh what the hell, give her my love."

Congress Street is the spine of Portland. It rides the crest of a long hill, trailing off through block after block of wooden tenements to a park overlooking Casco Bay. The extended neck of it ends, like a dinosaur's, in a tiny head, the red brick buildings of the Southern Maine Medical complex. The "deep throat" of Congress Street runs two blocks between the statue of Longfellow and the new art gallery. Kathleen's address brought me there, to the Xanadu Massage Parlor. I hung out across the street a while trying to decide what to do next. Hung out until a sports-jacketed fellow sidled up to me and asked did I like leather.

Like leather?

He leered at me. I could see his reflection wink in the smudged glass of the window. Over his head I could see UDANAX in pink neon tubing. Behind his face, behind the pink neon, in the window display I had been standing in front of, unseeing until then, were ten copies of *Leather*. The fly-specked sign above the display read "Adult Books."

I shoved my elbow in his ribs and started across the street, dodging taxis. We arrived at the door of Xanadu together.

"Sorry," he said. "I meant to pay."

"Glad to hear it," I extemporized. "I'm wired and this is a raid."

Inside a bored, middle-aged man said, "Sorry, sister, Krystal's not here."

"Krystal?"

"Yeah. Off Wednesdays."

"Off Wednesdays? Oh! No, I'm looking for Kathleen. Kathleen McGuire."

"Only Kathleen we got's Kathleen period and she don't do ladies."

"No. I'm a private investigator, looking for Kathleen McGuire. She's come into some money," I improvised. "Her sister in New York, this was the last address she had."

"Some money?"

"Yeah. An inheritance."

"Sounds like a scam to me," he said. But he put down his crossword puzzle book and disappeared behind the beaded curtains.

"No one knows no Kathleen McGuire," he said when he came back a few minutes later. "Been a while?"

"Probably."

"Try this lady," he said.

He handed me a scrap of paper toweling with a phone number on it. The pen had run out of ink and the figures were hardly legible. "Tell this Kathleen when you find her, I'm looking for a partner she has some money to invest."

My friend in the sports jacket had gone. I walked up Congress Street, off the strip, to McDonald's, and called Bruce McAntee. His wife answered. He was downtown at the *Stars and Stripes* office. No answer there. I tried the number on my piece of paper toweling.

The answering voice was throaty, velvety but rough, rubbed against the nap too long by cigarettes and whiskey. "What can I do for you?" it said.

"I'm looking for Kathleen McGuire," I said. "They gave me your number at the Xanadu."

"I don't know no Kathleen McGuire." The voice had lost whatever softness it had had.

"I have a message from her sister."

Silence.

"Her sister Sive?" I said. "Hey, it's real important I find her."

"Yeah, she inherited a fortune, right?"

"Not that I know of. I'm trying to find her son, Carlos."

"Wrong Kathleen McGuire."

"You do know where she is, though," I wheedled.

"Yeah, I knew a Kathleen McGuire once," the voice said grudgingly. "Had a sister Sive lived in New York. She didn't have no son named Carlos."

"Maybe not," I said. "But I'd like to find her."

"What's in it?"

"For her?"

"Yeah for her. For me too."

"A hundred dollars?"

She agreed to meet me at McDonald's in fifteen minutes. She said I'd recognize her, she had red hair. She did too. Bright red and lots of it. She may have been my age, but she looked a lot older. The address she had for Kathleen McGuire was old she said, and it was vague. "Sedgewick. That's up the coast a ways. She went with a guy by the name a Soper, Henry Soper. A million Sopers up that way, all related. One way or another. You'll find her. Don't worry."

While I waited for her, I had gone to the bank for a new one-hundred-dollar bill. She was pleased. "Long time since I seen one a them suckers," she said and smiled. It was a gummy smile but it brightened her face. I asked how she liked living in Portland. She shrugged and her smile faded. When I left she joined a man nursing a cup of coffee in a booth by the window.

Still no answer at *Stars and Stripes,* so I moseyed on down to Horse Feathers. I ordered a hamburger, asked the waitress for a piece of paper, and wrote Bruce a note. Said a lot had happened and I needed to talk with him. I didn't mention Georgie. I slipped the note under his office door.

I decided to keep the car I had rented and drive to Sedgewick, which is one of the hamlets scattered between Ellsworth and Bucksport and not far from Sister Pat's convent. I thought I would ask Pat to drive me to the airport again to return the car. I thought if I asked her to do that, she would invite me to spend the night. Thinking of spending the night with Pat, I bought a paper and checked the tides. If I hurried I could visit Clara on Monte Cassino. The thought made my heart beat funny and I wished I didn't have to walk all the way to Xanadu to get my car.

I left I-95 at Gardiner and made my way by back roads, past the Windsor Fairgrounds, to Route Three in China. Outside Belfast I stopped for gas at Murphy's.

"Got your Megabucks ticket yet?" the woman at

the counter asked. "It's ten million. Or more. More, likely."

I had two bucks and change coming after I paid for gas and coffee. "Sure," I said. "Why not." I said I'd pick my own numbers.

Over the years I had gone through every conceivable combination of birth dates in my family and of my fugitive loves. For a while I tried number anagrams of the letters in certain names; then in certain messages, like I love Pat. It was time to try a new tack. Four and ten, date of sobriety. Day one of a whole new life. One and seventeen. New life, period: my birthdate. Two more numbers. Ten and fourteen. Today, day one of the rest of my life. No good. Ten twice. Thirty-five, year I was born. Perfect! Bound to win. I dithered all the way to the convent about how I would spend my first million.

I discovered Pat in the barn milking Rosie the goat. Barney was away she said, in Connecticut. She would be glad to drive my car to the airport so I could return the rental, but I would have to bring her back home again.

"It's three-thirty now. You want to stay over?"

"I thought you'd never ask."

While she washed up, I paced the cloisters connecting the barn-like house to the house-like barn and daydreamed. It was getting too late to visit Monte Cassino in the flesh, so I went there in spirit. It was a lovely visit. Sr. Clara met me. She welcomed me with those amazing eyes. She said, "I was expecting you."

We spent my first million in no time flat, and then we spent it all again.

Pat said she called me three times before I woke up. "Where are you?" Pat said. "Hello?"

Coming home, we went through Blue Hill to Sedgewick. Pat suggested that we stop at Largay's outside of town. "Everyone shops here," she pointed out. "If anyone's going to know Kathleen, they will at Largay's."

And they did. "Kathleen Soper? Only Kathleen Soper I know lives down the road here. About two miles. Right before the bridge. It's a little house on your left. If you come to the bridge you know you gone too far."

Pat spotted it. Scattered in front were three rusted carcasses of cars partially hidden by tall grass and rugosa rose bushes ladened with swollen hips. The car bodies provided shelter for two beagles and a retriever on short chains. They seemed displeased by our visit. They weren't the only ones to seem displeased. A bearded man about ten feet tall with a shotgun under his arm stepped out on the porch.

"Don't go turnin' in our yard!" he shouted.

I rolled down the window. "We're not turning. I'm looking for Kathleen Soper."

"Ma!" he yelled.

Kathleen Soper looked different. Different from her sister Sive, and different from her friend in Portland. But she had abundant red hair, like her Portland friend, and the fine Celtic bones of Sive and Maria.

"Henna?" I asked Pat, the expert on henna, which she uses to make her own hair a brassy, unreal red.

"No way. It's a wig."

"Who you lookin' for?" the woman called.

"Kathleen Soper," I yelled out the window. "I've got a message from her sister, Sive."

"From who?" Kathleen started down the porch steps. "From who?"

I got out, being careful to stay clear of the straining, yapping dogs. "I been to New York. I saw your sister. How I came to find you. She sends her love."

By now Kathleen was only a yard or so away. "Her what?"

"Her love."

"Bullshit!" She turned and started back to the house.

"I wanted to talk with you," I called after her.

"Well, come along then," she said.

We entered into the kitchen. The ceiling was low and sooty as were the walls. Wood smoke and cigarette smoke mingled with the odor of apples and stale beer, mold, manure and sweat. The odor of poverty, Maine poverty, somehow duller than the sharp smell of it in San Miguelito. An old iron cook stove took up most of the room. A red hand-pump, the paint peeling, stood on the counter which held a dusty begonia and stacks of dirty dishes. The man with the gun had disappeared.

"Get you somethin'?" Kathleen asked. She held up her glass, the liquid in it was amber. She took a drag from the cigarette that lay smoldering on the edge of the counter. "Have a seat," she invited.

There were three chairs at a table beside the stove. Pat and I sat; so did she.

"Rollie, you get the hell back here with that

bottle," Kathleen yelled. "Kids!" she spat. "Nothin'
but trouble."

Above the table was a window into the room
beyond. A hand reached through holding a bottle of
bourbon.

"Keep your filthy hands off my things," Kathleen
advised. "You hear me? I said you hear me? You get
yourself out here, Rollie."

Rollie was in his early twenties and big — like
the man with the shotgun. I had seen him before.
Rollie was the volunteer out at Monte Cassino who
had taken the snapshot of Marie and me. The
picture Bonifacio had shown me at Tocumen airport
in Panama City.

Rollie looked uncomfortable — embarrassed
maybe. He looked as if he wanted to avoid my eyes
but couldn't. He shot staccato glances in my
direction. I said, "Hi, Rollie. How ya doin'?"

"Yeah," he said gruffly. He said, "Ma, I didn't
take your effing bottle. You had it watching TV."

"Don't talk back to me you little sucker, I'm your
ma."

Rollie's eyes rolled around in their sockets. "Yeah,
Ma. Tell me something I don't already know."

"Don't be no smartass neither."

"Ma," he said, "I'm goin' inta town. You want
somethin'?"

"Yeah, you can get me a bottle a Granddad like
this one you drank all of."

"Sure," he said. "See ya around," he aimed at the
space between Pat and me, then turned and left.

"Kids!" said Kathleen again. She reached over
and took two juice glasses from the dirty dishes on
the sink. She held one and then the other up to the

89

light. They seemed to pass inspection and she poured whiskey into them.

"I don't drink," I said.

"Sure you do," she assured me. "Mud in your eye!" She swallowed hers and lit another cigarette. "What can I do for you ladies?" she asked, eyeing my glass.

At first Kathleen maintained she had never heard of any Carlos nor of any Maria. But after she had finished my whiskey and started in on Pat's, she began to talk wistfully about the "little buggers." And then she started denouncing "damned S.O.B. Henry Soper that wouldn't let me have my babies." She paused, holding Pat's whiskey like an ice pack to her forehead. "Except for that sunabitch Rollie I mean."

"Who is Rollie?" I asked. "Is he your son? Yours and Henry's?"

"You wait till I get my hands on him, that sunabitch," she replied. "Where'd he go anyhow? And where's that sunabitch Henry?"

Henry was the bearded man who had greeted us. Kathleen remembered — he was out hunting birds. "All the sunabitch ever does. Weren't fer Rollie God knows where we'd be at."

I asked what she meant, but her mind had wandered elsewhere. I tried again. "Where would you be if it weren't for Rollie?"

She waggled the bottle at me. The liquid sloshed around in the bottom. "Mama mustn't tell," she said. "Rollie'll get mad at her. "Hey!" she confided, "You doan wan Rollie mad at you. Unh unh."

It had grown dark while we sat there. The fire seemed to have gone out in the cook stove. I tried to rekindle it, but the wood box was empty, empty as Kathleen's life. I offered to fill the wood box. There didn't seem much I could do for her life. Then we left.

We stopped at Largay's again. I picked up some Stouffer's lasagna for dinner. Pat said she had cabbage and carrots in the garden for salad. She bought a *Bangor Daily*.

Tony Brown had made the front page. His erratic electric energy had short-circuited. He was dead. Drug overdose, according to the paper.

I was suddenly enormously depressed. "I wish," I said, "I had taken some of Kathleen's liquid refreshment."

"No you don't," said Pat. "You're driving."

Chapter 8

I woke too early the next morning. From my
narrow cot I could see the moon, slouched on its
side, looking tired like me. A storm in the night had
lashed the last of the leaves from the trees. I
counted: from mid-October to mid-May, seven
months. Seven months until the new leaves came.
For seven months the earth would look dead. Seven.

Too early and too cold to get up. I put my head
under the covers, curled over and hugged my knees,
and waited, fetus-like, for Pat to start a fire.

I decided what I would do with my Megabucks was buy a little house at Rio Hato, right off the beach, where I'd gone when I was a kid, and I'd get a horse, and I'd never be cold, and the earth would never die on me again.

I must have drifted off to sleep. The images of Bonifacio and Kathleen were vivid in my mind when I became aware of the smell of coffee brewing and Pat humming "Tantum Ergo" downstairs. Bonifacio so vibrant and young looking, Kathleen so wasted. Both so poor. One so dead.

Outside the world shimmered, gold where the early sun stroked the frost, silver in the shadows. From the barn I could hear the rooster crow. He seemed pleased with the day, and, after all, so was I.

Over breakfast, I filled Pat in about the picture Bonifacio had shown me at Tocumen airport, the one Rollie had taken of Maria and me. She thought it was peculiar. So did I.

"If you want to catch Rollie," Pat said reluctantly, "he works out at Monte Cassino for Clara."

"I thought he was a volunteer."

"Well, whatever. He works there and not just Saturdays. And he does have to earn his living. Doesn't he?"

His living, and one for Kathleen, plus one more for Kathleen's good friend, the jug. "Yeah," I said. "I guess."

Pat offered to let me stay the night again. "Stay for the duration, if you like."

"The duration?"

"Well, until you find Carlos, or whatever it is you're doing."

* * * * *

Clara was standing where I had left her, at the
dock facing the mainland.

Her eyes lassoed mine from a distance and bound
them tight. She said, when I was close enough to
say it softly, "Welcome, Brigid, we've been waiting
for you."

"Yeah," I said. Then I asked, "You waiting for
someone? I mean, like someone else?" How could she
have been waiting for me? remnant intelligence
inquired.

"Not really," said Clara. She took my arm.
"Would you like to help me shingle?"

Would I.

Before we shingled, Clara suggested, we should
have a cup of coffee. Her room was part of the barn.
It smelled of manure, and soap, and cloves. I liked
how it smelled. A little wood stove made it cozy. In
a voice so soft it was sometimes hardly audible,
Clara told me how good God had been to the little
colony of Monte Cassino. I mostly said "Yeah" and
listened until she got to modern times.

"I hear that Carlos Pardo, or Chester Brown, was
last seen here on Monte Cassino," I put in.

She seemed to blush. She covered her face. When
she raised her head, her eyes took mine captive and
she said, "Rumors."

"Rumors," I repeated. I managed to look away,
and then I said, "Some people think Carlos is still
alive. That he runs drugs through here. That that's
how you got the money to build shelters."

She put her hand on mine. "Do you believe that,
Brigid?" she asked. I looked from her hand, the long,

strong fingers, the ragged nails, up to her eyes waiting for mine, waiting to escort me into that secret place I had once been to, and had longed for ever since.

My silence was the answer she wanted. She said, "They don't know what they're saying. Those people, they don't understand the poor. But God seems to think we're doing the right thing. And that's all that matters."

"Yeah, right," I said. Then I asked her about Rollie. "That young man who works out here. I visited his mother yesterday. What's the story there? It seemed like he supports that household. How do you manage to pay him?"

"God takes care of that," said Clara.

"God?"

"Rollie is a volunteer."

I asked who paid for Kathleen's Old Granddad.

Her hand on mine moved slowly back and forth, stroking. I liked the feel of it, her calluses, rough and warm, like the tongue of a cat. She said, "Ask him. He's around here somewhere."

"Well," I said. Then, "God has been good to you," popped out of my mouth.

For my reward, Clara squeezed my hand and said I could shingle the side of the new house. By myself. I said, "Thank you." But the problem of Rollie continued to nag at me. If Clara wasn't paying him for the handyman work he did at Monte Cassino, someone else was paying him for some other kind of work. And what could that be but running drugs? There wasn't anything else young Rollie seemed qualified to do. I hoped Monte Cassino wasn't involved. I hoped that Carlos Brown's suspicions had been wrong, that no one was using the flow of illegal refugees across the Canadian border to mask the flow of illegal drugs back in. I hoped that Clara was innocent.

About that time — Clara's hand still covered mine — the door burst open and in came Maria, seething.

"Where the fuck have you been?" she asked

Clara's hand dropped from mine and she covered her ears. She blushed again and she said, "Oh, Maria! Your language."

"Fuck my language," said Maria. "Where were you?"

Clara covered her face. From behind her hands, she murmured, "I forgot."

"No you didn't forget. Another butterfly crossed your path." Maria looked at me contemptuously.

Me a butterfly? That I resented. It must have shown.

"Don't worry," Maria reassured me, "this has nothing to do with you."

Nothing?

"Hey," I said, "it sounds like you two have things to work out. I'll just start shingling."

I had done one full line when Maria showed up. "I'll help," she said shortly.

"I can manage," I said.

"I said," she said, "I'll help."

"Yeah, right!"

After ten minutes or so, Maria stopped snorting and I ventured to start a conversation. "I met your mother," I said.

"Sive?" she asked, not very interested.

"Yeah. I met Sive. But I meant Kathleen."

That caught her interest. "How did you find out about Kathleen?"

So I began to tell her my adventures, retracing my route in response to her questions. When I got to Bonifacio's murder and the missing photographs, Maria seemed to stop listening.

I said, "Rollie's your brother, too."

"Too?" she said absently.

"Well, Carlos. Carlos and Rollie."

"Oh, right. Carlos."

Then I remembered that Tony, wired Tony, was also her brother. I said, "I heard about Tony last night. I'm very sorry."

She brushed away my sorrow.

"Where will he be buried?" I asked.

"Won't be," she said.

I thought about it. "Cremated?"

No answer. I asked, "What will you do with his ashes?"

She said, "I won't do anything with them. Dito is coming for the ashes."

Dito. I hadn't seen Dito Brown in forty years. I tried to recall him. All I could capture was the hazy memory of a slender youth, very handsome, lots of smiles. I asked, "Have you ever met him?"

"Are you kidding?" After a moment Maria said, "He's coming to the viewing this afternoon. At Mitchell-Tweedie's in Bucksport if you want to come. Clara offered to go with me to see everything was okay. I waited an hour for her. Why I was so upset. Sorry to involve you."

"No problem." Then I said, "You know, I've tried to find Carlos, like you wanted. Why I went to Panama."

Maria was standing on a ladder at the other end of the wall. She threw the shingle she was holding to the ground, then her hammer. She said, "I am sick to death of Carlos. He can stay right where he is and I don't give a damn if they never find him. I have got to go to Mitchell-Tweedie's."

As she passed by me she looked up, as if she were noticing me for the first time. She said, "I couldn't talk you into coming to Mitchell-Tweedie's with me? I've never done this before, and it's creepy."

Shingling Clara's wall was less exciting than looking into her eyes or holding hands with her. I said, "Sure, why not."

Walking up the road to the gravel spit, I spotted Robert Jardin talking with Clara by the barn door. I was surprised to see him. I waved and shouted a greeting. "I'm going to the funeral parlor," I cried to Clara. "Does he come here often?" I asked Maria.

"Who?" asked Maria. "Our friendly local druggist?"

"You don't like him?"

"What's to like."

Death had quieted Tony Brown. He lay looking as peaceful as Clara, his hands folded across his breast, as Clara often folded hers, as St. Theresa of Lisieux is shown folding hers in those catechism cards they give you with the thin gold border. Someone had laced a rosary through his fingers. Half a dozen sweetheart roses lay along his side.

On the way to Bucksport, Maria had said little,

and only when I asked a direct question. Like, "Why didn't your friend, Alex, come with you?"

"One of us has to work," she replied curtly. Then she said, "Alex'll come later. After four."

What Maria was so upset about was Dito coming. I tried to put myself in her shoes and found they pinched. She had never met her father. Never even seen him.

It was late when Dito got there, after seven. He came in with Robert Jardin. The Panama contingent. What a contrast! Robert, thin and ferrety, Dito more like a lion, barrel-chested and tawny, the skin of his face golden, his eyes, like his sister Georgie's, flecked with amber. Dito's hair had begun to gray, but it was thick and curly, and perhaps, like his lashes, a little long. He wore a pin-stripe gray worsted suit and wing-tip shoes. He was gorgeous.

He strode up to the coffin. He knelt and crossed himself in the intricate gestures Latins use. He clasped his hands, resting them on the edge of the coffin, and lowered his head in prayer. He remained there a long time. Well before he quit Tony's coffin, Maria got up and left through the front door. When Dito finished communing with his dead son, he rose, nodded to Jardin, who had taken a seat in the front row, and together they moved down the aisle toward the door. I intercepted them at the sign-in book.

"Dito?"

He looked down at me. He was a good deal taller than Georgie. "Yes?" he said, the "Do I know you?" implied.

"Brigid Donovan. Panama? Cristobal High School? El Valle."

Before I had finished my litany, a brilliant smile

replaced Dito's condescension. "Of course. Georgie said I might run into you. She sends her love."

I said, "Yeah."

"Jardin," said Dito, "find Sr. Clara." To me he said, "We're going to that little restaurant in town, Jardin says it's decent. Won't you come? Perhaps you've met Sr. Clara." He nodded over my shoulder.

Clara had changed her workshirt, you could tell: there was no cow dung on this one, and the spots of pitch, having been through the wash, were all dried out. But she still smelled of the woods and the barn. Not Joy Parfum, but I liked it.

"Sr. Clara has accepted my invitation to dinner," Dito said, "and I hope that you will, too. Jardin, bring the car around."

I shouldn't have accepted the invitation, but I liked McLeod's, especially their chocolate silk pie. Also, I was curious about the relationship between Dito and Jardin, and between Dito and Clara. For a crazy minute it felt as if I had been invited to a meeting of the Cosa Nostra: Dito so like a godfather, down to a discreet diamond ring on his right hand; Jardin, obsequious as a *consigliere*, Sr. Clara their improbable confessor.

The reason I shouldn't have accepted, though, was that I was too tired. If being distracted causes some people to speak the truth, being tired makes me stride into places any fool knows enough to steer clear of. Through most of the meal I didn't say much. Clara blushed and covered her face a lot, Jardin anticipated Dito's wishes, and Dito himself was gracious. Gracious and somber, as befitted a man who had just lost his only acknowledged son. His only acknowledged child.

The trouble started over dessert. I had chocolate silk pie. So did Dito, on my recommendation.

He said, "I haven't had anything this chocolate since I was a kid."

Clara took a bite of mine — she had declined dessert — and said, "Oh, Rollie brought this to community supper once. His mother made it."

I said, "Same recipe."

She said, "Come again?"

It was on the tip of my tongue to explain that Rollie's mother was Maria's mother, too. Kathleen McGuire, then a sweet young thing just arrived in Panama from Ireland, who had helped in the kitchen, got to make pie for the family upstairs, and pie for the young master who loved chocolate. Loved chocolate and other things.

What I did say was even worse. I turned to Dito and asked, "Who made the pie you remember?"

"She ironed for us," he said. "Her name was Bonifacio. She came from the interior, El Valle actually. You probably remember her, Brigid."

"I do actually. I thought maybe a woman named Kathleen had made it."

"No," said Dito, surprised and a little amused. "It was Bonifacio. I wouldn't forget something like that."

"Oh, Bonifacio made it. Now let's see . . . Bonifacio, that was Carlos's mother, right?"

"Carlos's mother?" Dito looked puzzled. Then his face cleared and he said, heartily, too heartily, "Carlos's mother. Yes, of course. Carlos's mother."

"You'd forgotten that," I said nastily.

Dito touched the linen napkin to his lips and said, "That was many years ago."

"Yeah," I agreed. "A lifetime ago."

Dito turned to Jardin and said, "Robert, the check."

Jardin, hollow-eyed and pale, rose and said, "I'm going outside for a cigarette."

Dito took it well, this defection of his lieutenant; he hardly stopped smiling for a second. He snapped his fingers and the waitress came running.

Outside, there was no Robert Jardin. His car, too, was gone.

"It seems," said Dito, "that we've been stranded. Poor Jardin. All this has been a great strain on him, too. Tony was his godson. Is there a taxi in this town?"

Mitchell-Tweedie, where my car was parked, was up on Elm Street, only three blocks away. I said I'd go get it. I suggested that Dito and Clara wait for me in McLeod's bar. They seemed to find that idea congenial. It was cold and it had begun to snow.

It snowed all night, fat wet flakes. Not much stuck to the ground. Just to branches. A slender birch inside the cloister had bent double under the weight of it. Pat was desolate. I said I thought it would spring back, eventually.

I asked her to drive with me to Sedgewick again to visit Kathleen. But she said she had too much to do. I told her I would try to get back soon and help her out.

"I could use a volunteer," she said with a smile.

Which reminded me of the wall Clara had promised that I could shingle. My smile cracked around the edges, while behind it I calculated tides.

"Unless," said Pat dryly, "you've thought of some other commitment."

"No, no! Not at all. Hey! Catch ya later."

"I'll expect you when I see you," Pat flung over her shoulder as she strode out the door.

The drive to Sedgewick took about thirty-five minutes, time enough to span the globe, to span a lifetime. Plenty of time to say, "Loving God in Heaven, your name is holy, your kin-dom come, your will be done, on earth as it is in heaven." To say, earnestly, "Lead me not into temptation and deliver me from evil."

I did all that on the drive to Sedgewick. I retraced my steps to Panama. I contemplated Carlos's life and Bonifacio's. I said my prayers. Reciting that part on temptation got me to thinking about Clara and the crazy effect she had on me. The new thing in twelve-step programs like AA, which I don't go to much any more, is love-addiction. I decided I was a victim of love-addiction. Anyone with half a brain could see Clara was poison. Poisonous to me as a dry martini. Unfortunately, she was also just as attractive. I decided I couldn't help how I felt about Clara, but I could help what I did about it. And I pledged to reform. No way was I going to let Pat down and go shingle for Clara. No way. Though, come to think of it, I could. I could cross over, shingle for Clara a couple hours, and be back in Surry by five. It was still plenty light at five. But I wouldn't. No way.

Dealing with my old pal and former drinking companion Ed Kelly had taught me that if I wanted something coherent from a drunk I should try to catch one early in the day. Kathleen wasn't what

103

you would call sober, but she was coherent. And she remembered me.

I found her curled on the sofa in the inner room watching the *Today* show. She was alone except for her buddy, Old Granddad. She offered to share him with me. I opted for a glass of water and fetched it myself, searching through the glasses on the sink until I found one I could see through.

Kathleen waved her glass at me. "Make yourself to home," she suggested.

The parlor, sooty and low-ceilinged like the kitchen, overflowed with magazines and newspapers, *The Inquirer, Penthouse, USA Today.* Everything — Kathleen, the cobwebs obscuring corners where walls and ceiling met, the electronic eye of the television set — everything seemed blanketed in a gritty film of ash and soot, as if the room had been enchanted eons ago and now everything in it waited for a prince, or David Copperfield, to come to the rescue with some kindness like a kiss. Not mine.

I decided to get down to brass tacks before Kathleen slipped entirely away. I said, "Kathleen, I'm looking for Carlos."

But Bryant Gumbel was saying something more charming. Kathleen nodded to him and said, "I'll drink to that," and she did. Bryant smiled agreeably and said, "I'll return right after these messages."

"I'll be here," said Kathleen.

"Kathleen," I said, raising my voice above the one urging me to listen to KISS 92. "I want you to tell me about Carlos."

"Sure, honey. What's to tell? He's a sonabitch. Just like his father."

"Where was he born?"

She looked at me, startled as a deer. She raised her glass to her lips. Her hand trembled. She looked at me over the rim of the glass, as if it were some bunker wall and could protect her.

"Kathleen, where was Carlos born?"

I should have kept still. My voice distracted her from terror. She slugged the whiskey and laughed. She said, "In a hospital. In a hospital."

"Where was the hospital, Kathleen?"

She tipped some whiskey into her glass. "Wan some?"

"No thanks. Kathleen, was Carlos born in Panama?"

She waggled the bottle at me. "For me to know and you to ask," she said, girlishly.

"Or was he born on the Riviera? Some place like Nice?"

"New York. We just said Nice. You know so much, what're you askin' me for anyway?"

Messages over, Bryant returned. Kathleen was fading fast. Probably time for her morning nap. I left, having got what I came for.

When I was fourteen and in love with Georgie, shortly after the summer of my lovesick spying on her in El Valle, she had gone abroad. Abroad. Sometimes still when I say the word, an atavistic cell in my brain, or in my heart, shakes loose the thrill of romance I felt when I first heard, "Georgie Hendryks has gone abroad for the winter."

To the Riviera she had gone and taken with her the maid Kathleen. But she had come back alone. I know, for many were the nights I had fallen asleep imagining that I was Kathleen, knowing that I would never have abandoned Georgie, as Kathleen had abandoned her. "Poor Georgie," they all had said, my aunts and Georgie's, playing bridge and gossiping. "That woman just up and left her, stranded, in Marseille of all places. Homesick, I guess. Went back to Cork."

So, Georgie had come home to Panama alone in the spring. She and I returned about the same time, I from my first term at St. Andrews in Costa Rica, in love again, this time with Sr. Anne, my American History teacher, and mistaken in the conviction that my crush was a vocation. I had spent that summer not with binoculars but with beads. Less fun, but I hadn't picked up tick bites as I had the summer before, lying in the grass looking for Georgie. And so I had collected no evidence to confirm that summer's gossip about Georgie's romance with Robert Jardin. It had been a foregone conclusion that they would marry. Mother was surprised the trip abroad hadn't been a honeymoon. Mother just couldn't understand it when the engagement ended. "Lover's tiff," had been her opinion. But as the months passed, and the rift began to seem permanent, I had decided that Georgie, like me, had discovered a vocation. My fantasies had begun to figure a trio of black-robed nuns — Sr. Anne, Sr. George, and Sr. Brigid — melting down romantic cloisters together, holding hands and chanting plainsong.

These memories for the most part amused me, in a tender sort of way. I thought I understood now what had happened that long ago summer when Georgie went "abroad" with her maid, Kathleen. They each had given birth to a child, Kathleen to Dito's Maria, and Georgie to Carlos, who was, apparently, Robert Jardin's child. I wondered fleetingly why Georgie and Robert had never married, and then decided that I knew.

Georgie had made arrangements for Kathleen to take both infants and to rear them in New York. No wonder Georgie had always shown such partiality to Carlos. He was hers.

Dito had not forgotten, the night before, who the mother of "his" child Carlos was; he had only forgotten, momentarily, what the lie had been. I thought about Robert Jardin's reaction. He must not have known. What a way to discover that he had a son — or had had one — because it seemed more and more likely to me that Carlos was dead. And I was sure that it was Robert Jardin who, that summer of my infatuation, had fathered Carlos.

For most of that long ago summer it had been only Dito and Georgie I saw together, riding, playing badminton. In the late afternoon sometimes they would dance for hours on the terrace together, jitterbugging, doing the tango. I had loved to see them tango. Then, around the end of August, Robert Jardin had appeared. Every weekend he would come, and while he was there, it was Robert Jardin that Georgie would dance with, and it had been Robert Jardin I had fantasized being.

I wondered what Jardin would do with his new information. I decided to drop in at his pharmacy in Blue Hill on my way back to the convent and find out.

I continued to muse over what I had discovered, what I surmised, and what I didn't understand. Most things fell under "didn't understand."

I had discovered that Maria and the missing INS man, Carlos Pardo, who had been brought up as brother and sister, were not. I wondered whether Maria knew, and I decided she didn't. I decided she must still think of Carlos as her brother. Why else was she so anxious to find him?

Maria's brother Rollie, now he was someone I wouldn't want to meet on a deserted street at night. What, I wondered, was he up to? Whatever, I knew it couldn't be good. Had he sent the picture of Maria and me to Georgie? And what was he doing out at Monte Cassino "volunteering?" Rollie and Sr. Barnabas, a bad combination.

Drugs. That was the only sane conclusion anyone could come to. But I stubbornly refused to believe that of Clara, though I wouldn't put anything past Barnabas or Rollie. On the other hand, how dim could Clara be not to know if there was something on Monte Cassino rotten enough to attract those two maggots?

Then there was Bonifacio's death to account for. Not to mention the attempt made on my life on that lonely road outside El Valle. For a moment, I lost confidence that Bonifacio's death was connected to Carlos's disappearance. Or that my accident was anything but an accident. Then I remembered the note placed in my pocket by someone in the crowd outside Bonifacio's door. For the first time I considered the possibility that it wasn't a threat so much as a curse, a way to wish me the worst sort of evil. Taking that line of reasoning, however, left unexplained Georgie's elaborate charade with the photograph album. Left unexplained why Bonifacio's beautiful young son wanted me to see the album after the pictures of Carlos had been removed.

Carlos. That's where it had all begun. I had to

find out what had happened to Carlos before any of it made any sense. It seemed that all of my questions were leading me to Monte Cassino, where Carlos was last seen, where Maria would probably be, where, possibly, I would even find Robert Jardin, my favorite pharmacist.

I considered my situation. It would take an extra half hour to go into Blue Hill to look for Jardin, and, I thought, he probably wouldn't be there anyway. Most likely, I thought, he was out with Clara again. I hung a right at Largay's and headed toward Monte Cassino.

What else could I do? It's not like I was going out there to shingle.

It had started to rain, a thin cold drizzle. The tide was low enough for me to drive across to the island and, since I didn't plan to stay long, that's what I did. On the other side, I came upon Rollie with a huddled group of refugees who looked cold and miserable. They seemed to be putting a fence around some recently mutilated forest land. Rollie hailed me.

"No one's up to the farm," he said, leaning through the window with his bushy beard and bushy eyebrows. His breath, too, was bushy, thick with frost and beer and onions.

"Where's everybody?" I asked.

"Funeral."

"I thought they were going to cremate him."

"Not Tony, friend of Clara's," he said laconically, then added, "Maria's up to the barn."

109

"Actually," I lied, "that's who I came to see."

Rollie withdrew his head and thumped the side of the car. "Care," he said.

Maria was into the Mass wine. I found her sitting by the stove in Clara's room. She offered me some. Then she remembered, "Oh, thas rye, you don't drink." And she dismissed me with her eyes and a wave of her hand. "She's not here, lucky for you. Hey! I wanna give you some good advice."

I didn't think Maria's advice would interest me. Especially not then. I said, "Sive told me when I saw her in New York that you had written her trying to find Carlos."

Maria shook her head. "Why'd I wanna find that son of a bitch for?"

"You wanted me to find him," I reminded her.

Maria shook her head some more. "You don't hear good," she said. "I want to know what happened to the son of a bitch. That's all."

"You mean you want to know if he's alive?"

"Oh, for Christ's sake, Carlos's been dead, he's been dead . . ." She started to count on her fingers, then gave up. "Oh, a long time. Two years in January whenever that is."

"Then why did you write to Sive?"

"For his bank. I wanted to find out did she know his bank."

After a while, I asked, "Why?"

Maria pulled her lips into a thin peevish line. She said, "I want the money."

"What money?"

It seemed that the income from the trust Georgie had established for the two children, Maria and

Carlos, was inheritable by their children equally, but if either died childless, the income was to go to the survivor.

"I wanted to know what the hell his bank was doing with his money," said Maria, " 'cause he sure as shit wasn't doing anything with it." She hoped they might be talked into transferring Carlos's income to her. But no such luck. "Wanted proof the S.O.B. was dead. Or wait a million years," she ended, grumpily.

"How do you know," I asked, "that Carlos is dead?"

"Well," she said, irrationally, "who isn't? Look at Tony, what happened to him . . . and Bonifacio. Look what happened to her!"

"Is that germane?"

"Germane!" she scoffed. "Yeah, it's germane."

I asked how she heard about Bonifacio and she said Tony told her. Then she suggested we go look for Carlos.

"You just said Carlos is dead," I reminded her.

"You don't hear good," she told me again. "I said less fine him." She drained her glass and leaned into my face. "You wanna hear the story or not."

I told her I did, of course. But I was skeptical that I would believe — or understand — what she had to say. I offered to make her some coffee. She said her wine was fine. I said, "Speaking of advice, I have some for you."

"Wassat?"

"AA."

"AA my ass!"

According to Maria, Carlos was most certainly

dead because Maria's partner, Alex, had spent a
weekend right here on Monte Cassino with his dead
body.

"Come on!" I said. "You expect me to believe
that?"

"Damn right. She wrote a book about it. Read
the book, you don't believe me."

I asked who had published it. "Nobody. Stupid
title, thas why. She said since everything in the
book was true she was gonna call it *Thoreau*."

"Come again."

*"Only One Thing in this Book Is True: I Never
Read Thoreau.* Now who's gonna publish somethin'
with a stupid title like that? I keep telling her, but
she likes it. We think Rollie threw the body in the
cedar bog. The one down by Immaculate Conception.
Wanna look for it with me?"

What had happened, according to Maria, on the
night of Carlos's planned raid of Monte Cassino, the
raid that had been aborted by an unpredicted
Northeaster, was that Alex had been trapped alone
on the island. Alone except for the body of Carlos
which she had come across lying crumpled at the
foot of the stairs down at Immaculate Conception,
his neck broken it seemed in a fall. Alex had got
through the nearly three days of storm by writing
an account of the events leading up to her
predicament.

"Come on," said Maria. "Less go find his body.
What's wrong, you scared?"

I hedged. "It's getting late."

"Don't worry about it. Clara won't be back until
really late. We got lottsa time to find him."

"You're drunk."

112

"No shit!"

I had misgivings about disappointing Pat, of course. But I could explain that Clara hadn't even been here. Not that Pat would listen to my explanations. I forgot all about the tide and the fact that my car was on the wrong side of the spit.

The hill down to Immaculate Conception was steep and badly rutted. Maria seemed to sober up, though, in the fresh crisp air, and, after falling once, maneuvered well enough. The trees on either side were sinewy hardwood, leafless and tall. They formed a vault far above us, the clean black tracery of their sky-high branches framing fragments of blue like the clerestory of an immense cathedral.

The cedar bog lay on our right. Entering it was oppressive, like entering a cave. Cedar branches grew together thickly, their lacy leaves embracing. Little light reached the ground which was spongy to step on and soon soaked my boots.

"Do you know where you're going?" I asked. But Maria, sure-footed suddenly and following a path that I could not discern, quickly moved out of sight. I asked her to slow down. She seemed not to hear.

I caught up with her sitting on a cedar log at the edge of a clearing where grasses and little flowers grew. I realized the flowers were carnivorous sundew, their innocent heads open for wandering insects to fall into. Others, heads closed, enjoyed their supper.

"Don't go in there," Maria warned. "You might not get out." She threw a rock. I watched it sink slowly out of sight. Carnivorous sundew, carnivorous bog, I thought.

"Is this where you think Carlos is?"

"Right."

"How do you expect to find him?"

"Good question."

The air smelled of death and corruption. Whatever Carlos's faults, like his macho patriotism and his hounding the refugees, this was a dreadful place to end up. I reminded myself that he had been dead before he landed here.

"Maria," I asked, "what did you think I could do?"

"You're such a hotshot detective, I thought you might be able to prove he was dead. That's all. Can't you see me telling the bank, 'Hey! My brother's at the bottom of this cedar bog so I want you to send me his money from now on.' Yeah, right!"

"Could they drag the bog?"

"Of course they can't drag a bog. Anyway, where would that leave Alex?"

"Why didn't she report it when it happened?"

"When the storm was over and she could leave, the body was gone. Who would have believed her?"

"So you didn't do anything?"

"What was there to do?"

How did I know? But I did know this: if Carlos was dead, he wasn't running a drug ring through Monte Cassino. Clara was innocent. But, I reflected, I already knew that.

As Maria got up to leave, we heard the sound of something heavy moving through the cedar toward us. Maria grabbed my arm and pulled me close to her. It reminded me of Susan, outside Bonifacio's apartment, when the hostile neighbors began to crowd us. Susan had taken my arm and pulled me close just as Maria was doing. "What's wrong?" I asked. Maria put her finger to her lips. She looked pale and frightened. "A bear?" I whispered. But she shook her head no.

Rollie broke through the brush into the clearing, a shotgun under one arm. "Looking at the sundews are ya, Maria?" he called.

Maria had said it was Rollie who dumped Carlos's body in the bog. If that were true, Rollie had even more to lose than Alex if the remains ever surfaced. I realized that no one knew I had come to Monte Cassino, and that my car was on the island too. I would only take a couple of hours to pull it apart. Then it could join Maria, Carlos and me in the bog.

"Those sundews really are something, aren't they," I began to babble. "Maria told me about them, I'd read about sundews, but I never saw one, she said would I like to and —"

"Shut up," Rollie said.

"Yeah," I agreed.

"What are we gonna do with you, Maria?" Rollie moved slowly forward until he was close enough to touch us. Maria shrank into the side of me. I shifted my weight to support her, finding it hard not to stagger.

"Don't you move none," Rollie spat at me. He prodded my chest with the barrel of the gun. "You wanna live."

A hot wave of anger carried me to some Never-Never Land where life and death have no meaning. I knocked the shotgun aside. "You fucking bully!" I raged.

Coolly he swung the gun at my head. I saw it coming in that same slow motion that I saw the road disappear from sight as my car sailed off the rim of the mountain outside El Valle. At first I felt nothing, just numbness and this ringing in my ears. Maria fell with me. I became aware of the blood as it filled the cup of my eye.

"Get up!" he said, "and march right on outta here. And don't you ever come back. Not unless you wanna stay."

Through the bog and up the steep track to the community, Rollie stayed right behind me, jabbing his shotgun every so often in my back. The pain in my head felt like a vise of heated metal wrapped around my skull from occiput to temple. Blood from the scalp wound continued flowing freely. "Maria, help me," I pleaded, but she had bounded ahead like something wild and wounded.

At the top of the hill, I sank to the ground. Pain had distorted the vision in one eye, blood had blinded the other. "I can't go any further without help," I said. Half expecting him to shoot, I was past caring. But he didn't even threaten me. There was only silence. Perversely, when I realized that Rollie, too, had gone, despair, thick like molasses, rolled over me.

Clara found me there, sitting on a boulder in the chill October twilight, bleeding — to death it felt like. She had a blanket with her. A good thing, I felt terminally cold. Strong arms lifted and carried me, Clara directing, and put me into a bed lined with warm bottles. I thought I heard her say, "Thank you, Rollie, I'll take care of her now." But I decided I must be hallucinating. I wondered whether I was dying on a boulder on Monte Cassino and this feeling of being cared for, of becoming warm again was just a trick my brain played to comfort me. I struggled to rise and save myself. I think I must have cried out for help.

"She's hallucinating," someone said.

"Yeah," I agreed.

Then someone started to wash my face and that's the last thing I remembered for a while.

Chapter 9

I spent the night with Clara. That's how I think
of it. Along toward morning, I woke enough to
realize where I was and why. Clara sat near me,
close enough to touch, if I wanted to. Her chair, a
plain wood kitchen chair, was drawn up to a rickety
table. She must have been reading, for her head lay
on an open book, her face in shadow from the
kerosene lamp burning low behind her.

My head throbbed, but not unbearably. I didn't
stir, wanting to absorb the moment, Clara's
closeness, the sense that my body had been taken

into that mysterious center where only my eyes had wandered before. I wanted to absorb the moment, and I wanted to prolong it, perhaps forever.

But she woke. Maybe she sensed my invading consciousness. She woke as though she had never been asleep, and she reached across to me and touched my face. She said, "You're awake."

I caught her hand. It felt rough, the texture of bark, and like bark it felt solid and warm, full of vitality, of life. "Hi," I said.

"How do you feel?"

I had an uncle, a rascal, who would have answered, "With my hands, you wanna be felt?" and then he would have laughed. I just laughed. A mistake. It made my head hurt worse.

She made me some tea and helped me to sit up in bed. A difficult patient, I had her adjust my pillows. I asked her to help me slip a sweater on. I asked her to look at my wound. I asked her to do whatever I could think of to keep her hovering near me, touching me with those powerful, long-fingered hands, so I could feel her and smell her.

Clara didn't smell at all like Georgie Hendryks. No Joy Parfum, no coral vine, no sickly sweet bouquet of gardenia and rose. Clara smelled of wood smoke and pine tar, of manure and of horse. She smelled to me of life.

I asked her who had brought me to her room.

"Rollie," she said. She said he had seen me and had called her. "Don't upset yourself," she advised, and she stroked my hair.

"Did he tell you what happened?" I asked. She made soothing noises with her tongue. I told her Rollie had hit me with the barrel of his shotgun.

"Poor Rollie," she sighed. My head began to ache worse. Clara said, "You've upset yourself, Brigid."

"Upset myself?" I said. Perhaps I was a little shrill, but I didn't yell at her, which is what she later accused me of. How could I have yelled with those hammers slamming around inside of my skull again? "Did I hear you say 'poor Rollie'?"

Clara withdrew her hands. She moved her chair back from the bed. She covered her face. Except for her body, she had gone.

"Clara?"

No response.

"Clara, Rollie's a bully. He knocked me down, he force-marched me up the hill, Maria's terrified of him."

Then Clara rose, and without looking at me, she turned and left the room.

I called to her, "Clara, come back. Clara, I'm sorry." But she didn't answer and she didn't come back. Pain kept me from going after her.

When it got light, I tested my legs. They felt like Jello, but they held me up. I had been on the island about twelve hours. With any luck, the tide would be out and I could drive across to the mainland. I used the closest out-house, the one without a roof, though it did have a door. I was glad it wasn't raining anymore. I couldn't find my keys, but I kept a spare one inside the front fender. It was 6:15 a.m. when I left. The spit was still under an inch of water. I didn't let that hold me up. I got to the convent a little after seven. I caught Sr. Pat milking Rosie.

She gave me the cold shoulder, as I had expected she would. But when Pat emerged from the gloom of the barn and caught sight of my blood-stained bandage, she forgot her resentment in very gratifying ways.

"Good God! Brigid, what on earth happened?" is how she began. Then she put her arm around my waist and propelled me down the cloisters into the convent where she settled me in the armchair under St. Joseph holding baby Jesus. She gave me tea and honey, and insisted on making me biscuits, and I began to feel better; both my head and my heart began to feel better.

When I finished telling my story she wanted to know what I planned to do next. "See Alex," I said and she approved, though she thought I should wait a day.

"Concussion," she fretted. "Let me see your eyes."

Her own diamond-shaped ones drew close to mine, but I could see their surface only. Pat's eyes didn't pull mine into them the way Clara's had. I thought of the rock Maria had thrown onto the bog. As irresistibly as it had sunk into the earth, I had sunk into Clara's eyes. Carnivorous bog, carnivorous sundew, carnivorous Clara. I started to giggle.

"See!" said Pat. "Into bed with you now!"

I was tempted. But at nine o'clock, after promising Pat I would come back to the convent for a nap at least, I set off for H.O.P.E. to find Alex.

Alex and a crew of munchkin carpenters were busy constructing another volunteer cabin. She looked fresh, quite unlike the night I had met her. She said to me, "Jesus Christ! You look like hell. What happened to your head? You run into a door?"

She took me back to the cabin she shared with Maria. But first she left instructions with her crew.

"No fights and don't come bothering me. You know what to do as well as I do. Better, probably," she added in my ear.

"You don't drink," she informed me when we reached the cabin, "and we're out of coffee."

"Water's fine," I said.

She handed me a mug. "The pump's outside."

I said I knew where the pump was. This woman sure could get under my skin.

When I returned with my water, Alex was drinking what looked like apple juice. It didn't smell like apple juice, though. I asked her about the weekend she had spent with Carlos's body at Monte Cassino. She offered me her manuscript. I said maybe later, but if she could just tell me the highlights.

The highlights were that she had gone to Monte Cassino in the storm after hearing on her scanner that it was about to be raided by the INS. Concern for Maria, who had been volunteering there that day, had driven her. She had searched the island, but no one seemed to be there. Ending up at Immaculate Conception, she discovered Carlos dead at the foot of a ladder-like stair leading up to the second floor. By then it was snowing too hard for her to leave. On the third morning, when she woke, the body had disappeared. She could tell by marks in the virgin snow that Carlos had been hauled away on a sled and taken to the cedar bog. Only Rollie, she said, was strong enough to haul Carlos through fresh snow three feet deep.

I asked her what she made of it. She poured herself some more of the yellow liquid. It came from an apple juice bottle. But it still didn't smell like apple juice, and she didn't offer me any. She said what she made of it didn't matter. I pressed her. She peered at me through the amber fluid like an alchemist calculating an experiment in transmutation.

"Clara knows," she said reluctantly. "Ask her."

"Clara knows what?" I asked.

"See, you're all pissed," she charged.

"Pissed! What do you mean, pissed!"

"See!" she repeated.

I decided I better let it go. I asked, "Would you like some water?"

"No. This apple juice is fine."

"I'll be back."

Outside the wind was sharp but refreshing. I pointed out to my Guardian Angel that I needed her. Then I took some deep breaths, and pumped another cup of water.

Back in the cabin I settled myself at the kitchen table again. My head had begun to hurt badly. I asked Alex for some aspirin. She wanted to know how I hurt myself.

"Didn't Marie tell you?" I asked, surprised.

"Nope. Does she know?"

I recounted my adventure with Rollie in the bog the day before. Alex didn't seem surprised. She said, "He'd do anything for Clara." I said I didn't see what Clara had to do with it.

"Wise up," Alex suggested. "And stop defending her. Won't get you anywhere. Believe me, I know. Did you tell Clara what happened?"

Reluctantly, I admitted that I had.

"See!" Alex jeered. "What'd she say?"

"She got mad."

"At Rollie or you?"

"At me," I admitted.

"Well then!"

Alex went on to tell me what happened when she confronted Clara after the storm. "See, Rollie served time a couple years ago, but he got an early release to Monte Cassino."

"Time for what?" I asked, interested but not surprised.

"He's real violent. When he gets mad. You're lucky. He wasn't what you'd call mad when he hit you, or else you wouldn't be walking around today. Probably shouldn't be anyhow."

According to Alex, Rollie worshipped the ground Clara walked on. "She says jump and he doesn't wait to ask how high, he's jumping as high as he can, and that's high."

"So you're saying what? That Clara knew Carlos was dead and told Rollie to dispose of the body?"

"Oh yeah. Definitely. She threatened me. See, I confronted her. I think she knew. You ask me, she was on the island the whole time — during the storm."

I asked what made her think that. It seemed to me Alex's resentment of Clara had clouded her judgment. The story she told of Clara's threats was incoherent. First she said Clara threatened her with a chainsaw, then she said Clara threatened to tell the police that Alex had murdered Carlos. "She's crazy," Alex concluded. "That woman is poison."

"Where Rollie is Maria's brother," I started to say, but Alex interrupted me.

"Rollie's *what?*"

"Maria's brother."

"No way."

I assured her that it was so and explained the genealogy. "Maria and Carlos were brought up as brother and sister. But she and *Tony* were brother and sister. Same father. She and Rollie have the same mother."

Alex looked dazed. She insisted I was wrong. "All wet" is how she put it. I assured her I was right. She said, "I've been with Maria, off and on, nearly twenty years. Don't you think I'd know if any of that was true?"

I said I didn't want to get into her relationship with Maria, but I repeated that what I had said was true. I invited her to ask Rollie's mother, Kathleen, if she didn't believe me.

"That drunk!" said Alex contemptuously.

"Yeah," I said. "That drunk."

That's when Maria appeared.

"Do you know what this . . ." Alex gestured toward me, "this asshole says? About you and Rollie?"

Maria said, "Brigid, why don't you take better care of yourself? You know, you probably have a concussion. I'd go to bed if I were you."

I said fine with me, but it wouldn't do her any good to tell Alex I was crazy and she, Maria, had better come clean, and other stuff like that. I was still babbling as Maria handed me out the cabin door.

Pat fed me when I arrived at the convent. Goat cheese with fresh dill mixed in it. Mint tea from the garden. Bread fresh from the oven. I said, "I like goat cheese."

"Chevron," she corrected me. Then she blushed. "Barney. We get a dollar more a pound calling it chevron."

I said, "Yeah."

I fell asleep in my little cot listening to Pat out back in the orchard. She was singing "Tantum Ergo" again. It's got a catchy tune. I woke feeling better and humming it myself. Pat said next thing I knew I'd be back in order again. I wasn't sure whether she meant my head or my soul. And I was afraid to ask.

Over some tea and bread and honey, we discussed what my next move should be. Pat thought I should "get to the bottom of this nonsense and find out what Clara really knows." Unwilling to stir up bad feelings between us again, I just said, "Yeah." She did agree that I should get in touch with Bruce McAntee, and after tea, I called him at *Stars and Stripes*.

He seemed distant. He said he couldn't talk just then. He offered to meet me the next morning in Portland. "In the office. At nine?" I said that would be fine.

It was getting on toward four o'clock. Pat said I should spend the night, get to bed early. She said she would get me up in plenty of time to make my nine o'clock appointment with Bruce. But I felt restless. I said I thought I'd be on my way. She said, "Well, you *will* spend tomorrow night here." I said sure, and then she said she would fix us a *coq-au-vin*. "Bartholomew," she sighed, "he's pecked me for the last time. We'll have Bartholomew." I wished she weren't on a first name basis with dinner.

It was forty miles out of my way to nip up to Blue Hill, but I wanted to see Robert Jardin. Looking back, I think it was guilt that drove me. Guilt that the only feeling I could muster for the man was a mild contempt. Even in Panama he'd been an outsider, his parents immigrants pushing their son up the ladder of class in a place where race weighed more heavily than cash. What I wanted to feel for him was pity, or at least compassion. I wanted to say to him that I knew what he must be going through, having lost a son, a son he hadn't even realized was his. I knew I could never do that, but I needed to express some sort of human concern, not for Robert Jardin, but for myself.

It was almost five and closing time when I walked into the pharmacy. It was quaint, an old-fashioned soda fountain along one wall, and long shelves with blown-glass bottles containing colored lotions, soaps and pastel powders. It had a pampered smell. Jardin was waiting on a customer, so I picked up a Blue Hill Packet and started to thumb through it. On page two Clara's face sprang out at me, her eyes boring into mine. My face was hidden when Jardin approached behind the bar to say he was sorry but the pharmacy closed at five.

Reading about Clara, the stories of her miraculous cures, of her good works, I had lost track of where I was. Lowering the paper, expecting maybe the Angel Gabriel, I saw instead an insignificant little man, balding, his cardigan raveling some at the elbow, his Adam's apple working. I said, "I'm sorry." He said, "Brigid, what the devil!" The departing customer said, "Care" in a voice I knew but couldn't place. I turned, but he had gone.

"Sorry," said Jardin. "I didn't expect you. How can I help?"

I muttered something about being in town and not wanting to leave without saying hello.

"Not going to Panama again?" he joked.

"No, Portland, as a matter of fact."

"I guess you can trust the water there."

"Yeah," I said. Then I blurted, "I'm sorry I didn't get to say good-bye the other night."

He brushed it away. "I'm the one to apologize. I took sick. Dito tells me you chauffeured for me."

"Yeah." I said I'd seen him out at Monte Cassino. "You go there much?" I asked.

He looked at his watch. "If I don't lock up, I may get another customer."

I said I had to be going. He didn't try to detain me. I asked again, "You know Clara well?"

"Sr. Clara? Our own Mother Theresa."

It didn't sound ironic. On the other hand it wasn't an answer to my question. He held open the door. "Drive carefully," he advised.

"Yeah," I said.

I left feeling dissatisfied, dissatisfied with Robert Jardin and dissatisfied with myself. Mostly with myself. I seemed to go around asking a lot of questions, but the only answers I got were ones people wanted me to have. And that wasn't the only problem.

When I'd solved the mystery of Sr. Pat's missing nun, people were all the time giving me a run-around. I decided then I just looked gullible: fifties, gray, tennis shoes. Who could blame them, I conceded at the time. But with that case, I had been emotionally detached. Except for Pat, and my old pal Ed, I could have cared less about anyone who was involved. The violence that had erupted like a volcano to destroy the foundations of those lives had meant nothing to me. I had easily detected the duplicity and the manipulation practiced by the major players and dealt with them accordingly. My detachment, I now realized, had protected me. That margin of safety was absent in this case.

I wanted too badly not to believe what people, what Alex especially, said about Clara. That she was involved with Carlos's disappearance, that she had spent the time of the blizzard out on Monte Cassino and kept that a secret, that she had told Rollie to dispose of Carlos's body. And I certainly didn't want to consider the possibility that she had used Carlos's disappearance to hide drug distribution from Monte Cassino, and that she used the refugees to disguise the bringing of drugs into Maine.

If the compass point of my judgment was in error because of my attraction to Clara, there was aberration also in my new antipathy to Georgie. I decided what I needed was a polestar to navigate by. But I wanted my star to be Clara, despite knowing in my gut that the light in those eyes was treacherous, and that it would, if I followed it, shipwreck me. I couldn't continue to discount evidence of Clara's guilty knowledge and possible involvement. Nor could I rely on a solution that rested on the assumption that Georgie was guilty. I wanted too badly to believe that Georgie had used her position as matriarch of the Hendryks family holdings in Colombia to build a drug empire.

And there were things I felt so guilty about that I knew my judgment was unreliable. I felt guilt for Bonifacio's death, a guilt that went deeper than my recent brief encounter with her. Guilt with roots as deep as the hatred Bonifacio's friends had expressed toward Susan and me. Colonial guilt, racial guilt, guilt so heavy I simply sank under it. Guilt that left me blaming others for a burden I couldn't carry alone. Blaming Dito especially. My contempt for that suave godfather-like figure because of his treatment of Bonifacio, of Kathleen, of Maria, left me convinced of his villainy. Georgie and Dito. Culprits. End of case. How and why didn't interest me.

Finally there was that niggling guilt that I felt about Robert Jardin. What a jerk! And I wanted to be able to take him seriously, I felt so sorry for him. But however deep my pity, my judgment, formed in the distant past of my adolescence, remained constant. Bobby Jardin's a jerk. Constant as a polestar, I thought ruefully.

I ended up at the spit again. The tide was out. But this time I parked the car and walked across. My smothering heart seemed to have invaded my lungs, and I could hear it beating in my ears. My palms inside my jacket pockets felt moist. I realized I hadn't grown up a bit since that summer in El Valle looking for Georgie Hendryks through field glasses. I realized, hopelessly, that I didn't want to grow up, that my long spell of grown-upedness, that tedious string of twenty-four-hours I had strung together since my sobriety had begun, was tasteless and uninteresting. Whatever else she was, Clara didn't bore me.

And she had forgiven me! She stood by the barn, leaning on a pitch fork, watching my approach. When I reached earshot, she said in that low sweet voice, "Welcome, Brigid. How is your head?"

She asked me in for tea, said she'd just done feeding the "hosses." She offered me bread. It lay on a plate in the window, dry and bearded. I declined.

The bed was turned back as I had left it. I wanted passionately to crawl back in, to put back the clock to when Clara had been hovering over me, to take back the words that had driven her in anger from the room. It was growing dark out.

"Can I borrow a flashlight?" I asked. "To get back."

"You just got here," said Clara, amused, reminding me of how much I had amused Georgie.

"Clara, they're saying Tony died of bad dope. Where do you think he got the stuff?"

Her kerchief was awry and a rope of red brick hair hung exposed across her cheek. Her familiar smell, earthy and sustaining, filled my lungs and quieted my heart. Her head drooped low from her neck as if she were meditating — or about to doze off. I said, "I feel so sorry for his dad."

She said, "Amen."

"Yeah. Amen. Who did Tony hang out with that might deal?" I persisted, determined to get some answers. "Was it someone here at Monte Cassino, do you think?"

131

She said, "Rollie."

She looked up at me, her eyes big and welcoming. I wandered into them a distance. I said, "Rollie."

"Poor boy," she murmured. This time I knew better than to respond.

I invited her to tell me more about poor Rollie. "I met his mother," I said to be helpful.

"Poor Kathleen," said Clara. Rollie, she told me, had been getting into scrapes from the time his legs were long enough to reach the pedals of a car, and that was young. "Eight I think. He was always a big boy, but they didn't send him to the youth center the first time. Maybe that was a mistake. His mother was no help, even a foster home might have been better."

Until he was eighteen or so, all Rollie's crimes had sprung from his lust to drive. He really had had no choice, Clara said. Even if he could have bought a car, Rollie had never learned to read. Any leeway for illiterates the law allowed would not have been given to Rollie, said Clara. "The town always had it in for them, Kathleen and then Rollie. You know how small towns are."

So, when the urge overpowered him, Rollie would take a walk into Blue Hill and find himself a car with keys in the ignition. "No harm in it," said Clara. "Even the police knew that. But what could they do. Tourists don't much like having their cars borrowed. And town folk hated Kathleen." Here Clara buried her face in her hands.

I asked why people hated Kathleen so. "She seems pathetic," I said.

Clara laid her hands out flat on her thighs, but

she kept her head lowered. "Now, yes. But ten years ago even . . ." Her voice trailed off.

Clara sat hunched. Looking vulnerable. I desired to protect her.

Clara's back curled like a wall surrounding a secret, a wall that I desired to breach. Torn between desires, I too sat silent. Unlike me.

After a time, Clara sighed and drew herself erect. "Well," she said, "it's getting late." The room was in such gloom I rather sensed than saw her. "Did you bring your car across?" She lit the stub of a candle standing in a saucer, moored in its own wax.

"Not this time. Did Kathleen set up a business here?" I asked.

Clara's hands covered her face again.

"I got her address from a woman who worked with her at the Xanadu, a massage parlor in Portland."

After a spell Clara's hands came down. She said, "Would you like to have supper with me? I have a casserole. From our community pot luck on Saturday. It's good food."

"I want to go to bed with you. I would be willing to go to hell with you. But eat your casserole? No way," I said to myself. Aloud, I hedged, "No, I can't. I'm sorry. Thank you."

"It's good food," she repeated.

I said, "I'm fasting."

"Oh, I see," she murmured and the sound gratified, like praise whispered in my ear.

"How did Rollie end up doing big time?" I asked.

"It wasn't his fault," she assured me. "He was just playing around. The way boys do."

"How's that," I asked.

"Happened at the Blue Bird Tavern down to Belfast. It wasn't the first time, that was the problem. And one of the people was from away."

Translated, I discovered, this meant Rollie was in the habit of getting drunk and violent. His pals never pressed charges; probably afraid to, I thought. But this time a man passing through had been messed up a bit. He didn't have to live with the consequences of Rollie's resentment and he did press charges. Rollie got out of Thomaston about the same time the fellow was discharged from Eastern Maine Medical, in a wheel chair.

Clara reached her casserole down from the shelf overhead and began to pick at it. "Sure I can't tempt you," she asked. I told her no, I didn't think so.

"When did Rollie start dealing drugs?" I asked.

"After that," she replied promptly. "He made connections in Thomaston. In a way it was better," she said in a considering voice. "Before, he stole, just shoplifting. People were afraid when he got out of Thomaston he'd be holding places up with a gun."

"Maria's afraid of him," I pointed out.

Clara pushed away her casserole as she might a naughty child, reluctantly. "Maria!" she said sorrowfully. "Poor Maria. She was afraid of Tony, too. And she was afraid of Carlos. I'm afraid Maria is afraid of men."

"Why would that be?"

Clara looked inquiringly at me. I say inquiringly. It was too dark to see her eyes, but her head was tilted and even though I couldn't see them I could feel her eyes probing mine. I realized that I had stumbled on the way to talk with Clara. I had to resist my urge to babble up her silences. I waited.

"Abandonment?" Clara offered finally.

"Abandonment?"

"Dito."

It was said so softly that for a moment I didn't realize that she had spoken. "Then you know?" I asked.

She said, "Poor Maria."

"Alex didn't know. They've been together, Alex says, for almost twenty years."

"Off and on," whispered Clara.

"That's what Alex said, off and on. You must know Maria well," I said, mincing my words because each one cut my heart.

"Maria has been very good to our community," said Clara, evasive as a summer breeze.

"Yeah." My stomach made a rude noise. I coughed to cover it. I wondered about the casserole, but decided I could hold out a while longer. "Alex thinks you were on the island that weekend when Carlos disappeared."

Clara said, "Poor Alex."

"Poor Alex, poor Maria, poor Rollie, poor Kathleen. I wish I knew what you really think."

Clara's hand covered mine, open on the table. I said, "Please don't say 'Poor Brigid.'" She sighed. I said, "Last night, Clara, when I told you Rollie was the one who hit me, you got angry. Why?"

"I wasn't angry," she said.

"You walked out of here like you were angry."

Her hand tightened on mine for an instant and then she withdrew it. "You were in shock," she said softly. "Maria called me," she lied.

"Yeah," I said. "Well, I gotta get to Portland. Can I borrow that flashlight?"

She said she would drive me across in the truck. She said the tide had turned and I would get wet otherwise.

We made the journey in silence. Clara silent from policy, and I by the skin of my teeth. If my heart had beaten with lust on my arrival, departing it beat with a frustrated rage. It was bad enough that Clara had evaded every question she didn't care to answer, and had cast doubt on the reliability of both Alex and Maria. What burned me was the knowledge that if I were to question her she would treat it like *lèse majesté* and dismiss me. The only way to stay on this woman's good side was never to cross her.

I felt like a monkey, the one who gets caught with her hand in the peanut jar. Caught because she's too greedy to let go. My jar was Clara's eyes. My brain knew I wouldn't find any peanuts there, just empty space to get lost in. But I needed to look. My rage was at the price of admission. Submission.

At that point I could just as well have spent the night in my cot at the convent listening to Pat sigh through the wall between us. But my heart was sore and ready to be wounded. Afraid I would take my frustrations out on her, I sailed past the turn-off and headed south on Route One. I gassed up at The Gateway in Bucksport. My stomach, complaining like a disappointed lover, I tried to silence with coffee. It was a good two hour drive to Moody's and I hoped to get there before they ran out of meatloaf. I told my stomach this, but it continued to berate me.

I arrived at *Stars and Stripes* a little before nine the next morning. Bruce, already there, looked tall, handsome and well-groomed, even his cowlick. I tried to smooth my own hair. Something about the way I'd slept had left it standing erect on one side. I would have showered, but the water in the cabin was cold and the air colder. Too bad. I said, "How's it going?"

The room looked different. Bruce seemed different too. But I couldn't put my finger on the difference. Disturbed, I started to chatter: Long time no see; Susan sends her love; What've you been up to?

He cut me short. "Sit down."

I realized the Macintosh was gone and the desktop was clean and dusted. The shelves running along the wall had been filled with neatly stacked notebooks and law books. The blue wall still was blue, but Ronnie had disappeared. The worry balls of dust were nowhere to be seen. For them I grieved. They had seemed somehow to trap the secret significance of life in their insubstantial toils.

Bruce said it was high time I was debriefed. I said I had tried to get in touch.

"Try isn't good enough," he said cool as a disappointed football coach.

"Hey, look, Bruce, I said I'm sorry."

"Sorry isn't going to keep you alive."

I said, "Come again."

He said, "Do you deny that an attempt was made on your life?"

"Two." It just slipped out.

"Two!"

A look of genuine alarm spread across his face, starting with the eyes. I realized he cared. That was all I needed. I blurted out my story, telling it backwards beginning with the recent encounter with Rollie in the Cedar Bog. By the time I had made my way back to Georgie's bedding me I had lost my resentment of Bruce for having manipulated me there. He kept making these little clucking sounds of sympathy and nodding his head. If I had had an older brother to stand by me through life, I imagined, he would have responded as Bruce did to my "debriefing".

During the course of my story-telling, Bruce explained the changes that had taken place in the office. "Mary, the wife. Said the place was a filthy mess. With Carlos gone, might as well give it a cleaning, and she did."

He also became something like the old Bruce as I talked. At the end he asked me, "Would you like a comb?"

"Won't do any good," I said, palming my unruly hair. "Need a shower."

"Oh," he said. Then, "When can you go back?"

I told him I planned to turn right around. "Pat's expecting me for dinner," I said. "I never did find out what Sr. Barnabas finds so interesting in Monte Cassino."

"No. I meant back to Panama."

"Panama!"

"Bob thinks you should, and I agree."

"Bob's your Uncle?"

"Come again?"

"Bob who?"

He looked surprised. "Robert Jardin."

"What does Robert Jardin have to do with anything?"

Bruce for a moment lost his bland self-assurance. "Er," he said, "Bob is part of the operation."

"What operation?"

"Operation Honorable Cause. You mustn't talk about it," he hurried to add. "I mean, forget I said it. Forget you heard me."

"Sure," I agreed. "Forget Robert Jardin, too?"

"It's not funny, Brigid. Look, Robert is CIA. The DEA is cooperating with them to get to the bottom of this drug trafficking through Maine. That bum Noriega, he's responsible —"

"You want me to go to Panama and bring back Noriega!"

"Brigid, what's gotten into you? This isn't funny."

"You're telling me," I said.

Bruce became persuasive. He had to, to convince me. Robert Jardin, that dusty little man with Bela Lugosi eyes and Andy Rooney brows, a CIA agent? Not even Graham Greene could have imagined an agent so unlikely. Besides, wasn't Jardin busy in his drugstore? Maybe the Company paid that deferential young clerk to run the store and provide Jardin's cover. Bruce talked earnestly most of the morning. By noon, we both were hungry, and we both had cowlicks. He called down to Horse Feathers for hamburgers and strawberry cheesecake.

What he wanted was for me to be a decoy. He asked didn't I think it was odd how Bonifacio had my picture and happened to see me at the airport.

"That was a setup," I said.

"Who set you up?"

"Georgie."

"But who sent Georgie the picture?"

"Rollie?" I hazarded. "He took it."

"Rollie!" said Bruce scornfully.

"So tell me," I suggested.

Bruce said they weren't sure, of course, that's why they needed me. But they had Maria and Rollie both under surveillance and they would nail whichever one made a move to inform Georgie. I said it seemed unlikely to me that either Maria or Rollie could be very high up in any international drug cartel. Bruce got self-important and told me to leave operational strategy to the experts. I must have looked mulish. He relented enough to say, "Don't you think if we have those two under surveillance we'll know who gives them orders?"

I declined to answer. Instead I asked another question. "What about Clara?"

"Sr. Clara? What about her?"

"Clara's not a nun," I corrected. "Sr. Pat, she is a nun, she thinks Clara's involved in running drugs."

Bruce snorted. "So did Carlos. Naw, she's okay. Robert vouches for her."

"Is that," I asked, "why he hangs out on the island?"

"Hangs out?"

"Well, I've seen him there."

Bruce smiled.

I told him Robert Jardin wasn't my idea of a CIA agent. Bruce smiled at that too. He smiled at a lot I said. He didn't smile when I told him about the note that had been slipped in my pocket at Bonifacio's apartment. He asked me to repeat it. He wrote down what I said.

Go home. Now. Never come back. How do you think it will feel to have a bat sewed up your puta cunt?

I told him what words to underline. He asked, "How do you feel about this?"

"How do I feel about it," I said mockingly. "Now let me see."

For a moment Bruce's self assurance slipped and something like alarm cast a shadow across his eyes. "Are you afraid?" he amended. You could see "the wife, Mary," had tried to do something with him. But even genius needs something to work with.

I thought about his question. "I was," I admitted. "Very afraid. Now it seems unreal."

"Oh, it's real enough," Bruce sighed. He rose from his chair. He turned and stood looking out the window at the drab rear walls of the buildings opposite. The sun had a frosty ring around it.

"Looks like snow," I said.

Bruce clasped his hands behind his back. Crisp copper hairs curled bright and clean on the knuckles of his hands. His wedding band looked newly minted.

"Wouldn't want anything to happen to you," he said to the sun.

"Yeah," I agreed. "Thanks. What do you want me to do once I get to Tocumen?"

"You can stay at a hotel. In Paitilla."

Paitilla, the ritzy new section of Panama City,

built by foreign capital for themselves and their playmates. The thought of staying at a hotel in Paitilla made me laugh. They'd tell me to use the service entrance if I started in the front door, me and my flea market specials. Bruce also seemed amused. He said, "Er."

But I thought about it. Paitilla might be a gas. If I didn't feel too uncomfortable. I might even ask for money to buy some new clothes.

Bruce said he thought it would be easier to keep an eye on me in Paitilla.

"Keep an eye on me?" I asked. "How long do you want me to stay there?"

"Oh, not long," he said.

"How long's not long," I wanted to know. "To be a decoy."

He said how could he know, but it wouldn't be more than a day or two. I said I thought he only wanted to find out whether it was Rollie or Maria sending messages to Panama, and who their boss was. He said that was so, but you never could tell. Tell what, I asked. He said if I had misgivings I shouldn't bother. He said that Honorable Cause would wait for another person as well-suited as I for the job, though God knows when that would be. He said his mother would never forgive him if anything happened to me. And did I think he would ask me to do something if he thought it would be dangerous, really?

He shot back his cuff and looked at his watch. He said, "Excuse me, Brigid, I had scheduled you for some training starting this afternoon." He held up his hand, "I know, I know. I shouldn't have assumed you'd want to go along. But I need to call and cancel. They'll be waiting."

It's not like I didn't know he was manipulating. And the reason I agreed to go wasn't his guilt-tripping. Truth is, I just wanted to. Whatever doubts I had were overcome by the enticement of training. Brigid Donovan, Agent.

So I signed up for a week's worth of training and a thousand dollars worth of new clothes. Bruce scheduled the training to begin the following Monday. I called Susan. She didn't seem too disappointed I wouldn't be staying with her. But she said whenever I came, she would meet me at the airport. I said I'd take her out to dinner. Her and Frank. In Paitilla.

Chapter 10

I didn't leave for Panama right away, not until late November. It looked as though I might be there for Thanksgiving. I wished I could be there at Christmas. A day or two before Christmas the Trade Winds start to blow. The rain stops, the humidity overnight is gone. Everything rustles with new life, new hope. I could decoy my way up to Rio Hato one day and swim.

As it was, I would be there at the dreary end of rainy season. At least it would be warm. Too warm. Pat said you couldn't please me. Pat said I was either complaining about how cold it was in Maine or complaining about how hot it was going to be in Panama.

"Come with me," I said, "and I promise never to complain again." She just laughed.

Barney came home and so I left the convent. Pat said, "No need to, Brigid. You're welcome to stay here." But I thought she had me measured for a habit, the kind I didn't want, and so I left. But not before making a few farewell visits in the neighborhood.

I called Robert Jardin and we arranged to have lunch at the Left Bank in Blue Hill. He arrived looking drowned. I must have looked drowned, too, but he looked like a drowned rat. He'd grown a mustache since I'd seen him last. Unlike his bristling brows, it was wispy and wet. Not your usual image of a CIA man.

Since he knew anyway, I told him I was going back to Panama. Bruce had told me to keep the trip under my hat until the last minute, but Jardin didn't seem surprised at my announcement. He asked where I'd be staying. I told him Paitilla. Somewhere. Bruce was making the arrangements.

"Bruce?" he asked.

"McAntee."

"Of course," he said.

He recommended the onion soup, so I ordered that. "The bread is excellent, have a sandwich," Jardin urged. "In this weather, you need all the help you can get."

He asked whether I had seen Maria recently. I fingered the healing wound at my temple. I said not for a few days.

145

He began a rambling account of the aborted raid Carlos had launched against Monte Cassino. "Maria was there, of course," he said.

"At Monte Cassino?" I was curious. "How do you know?"

"They lived above the store," he said. "She and Alex. Wasn't much I didn't know about their comings and goings. Days." He smiled. "Walls're thin, so's the floor." Whatever he had heard had amused him.

Maria had spent the day out at Monte Cassino volunteering her labor. She had only recently moved to Maine and didn't have a job. "Spent her days painting. Then, after she met Clara, she'd go out to Monte Cassino and work, especially when the weather was bad. Couldn't paint then. Not her kind of painting."

Jardin delivered his story in a leisurely ramble throughout lunch. It was punctuated by other diners who stopped to chat, to tell him how some prescription had worked, about a new grandchild, their bravery hunting deer. He seemed to know everyone in Blue Hill. He would, I guess, being the only druggist.

On the night of the raid, the night the famous three-day blizzard began, Alex had been upstairs fixing supper. "She had the scanner on. Couldn't make out what was being said, but you could hear the calls going out. Then all of a sudden there's a crash like she knocked over a chair and away she flies like a bat out of hell. I turned on my scanner to find out what it was she heard. They were talking about the raid on Monte Cassino."

Picking through his salad, looking under each lettuce leaf, searching perhaps for a fuller understanding of the events he was relating, Robert explained that he had spent the first night of the storm in the drugstore. "The lights were out, of course," he said, studying the aduki bean caught in the tines of his fork. "So no one could tell I was there. I suppose." The aduki disappeared under the sparse black foliage of his lip.

I had long since finished my own lunch. So had everyone else. The waiter, no doubt familiar with Robert's pace, had disappeared into the mysterious heart of the restaurant.

Robert continued in his languid way to describe the scene. "The stairwell to the upstairs apartment passes alongside the wall of my office. About an hour after Alex left, I heard Maria come in. She had a helluva time getting that outside door open."

Once in, Maria had collapsed, weeping on the stairs. Robert had gone to her. She was so distraught he had been afraid to leave her. Maria, he said, was so upset because she had just killed her brother, Carlos.

"Come again?" I said, having heard but not believed.

"Yes. That's what she told me. I was inclined at the time, of course, to think she was just being hysterical. Johnny! Another Bock, please," Robert called toward the kitchen door. A moment later our pony-tailed waiter appeared with a beer and a frosted glass. Robert carefully wiped his mustache clean of luncheon detritus.

"Well," I said impatiently as soon as the waiter had gone, "what did you do?"

"Do? Nothing. What was there to do? I think you scarcely appreciate what that storm was like. No one

was out in it, believe me. Well," he corrected
himself, "that's not altogether true. Just about the
time I had Maria calmed down, one of the nuns
from the island, a Sr. Anne I believe her name was,
came in. She had a family of Guatemalans . . . or
were they Salvadorians? No, Guatemalans. They
were from the Altiplano, I remember the father
telling me that."

Sr. Anne had left the family with Maria and
gone on. Robert understood she had other refugees
with her and they were planning to stay at the
motel a mile out of town. "I never thought they'd
make it," he said. "But apparently they did. Anne
was driving a four-wheel-drive pickup. I remember
that. Even so," he said reflectively, remembering, I
guess, the wildness of the storm.

I found his detachment odd and irritating. I
asked what happened after the storm. I asked why
he had never said anything. His answer was much
like the one Maria offered me the afternoon we sat
side by side contemplating the cedar bog where,
according to Maria, the bones of Carlos lay.

"What would I have said?" Robert asked. "They
never found the body. All I knew was hearsay. I did
talk to Maria. Would you like some coffee?"

I did. On Robert's recommendation I tried a
raspberry turnover.

"You know," said Robert, cutting his tart into
bite-size pieces, "Maria was terrified of Carlos. You
did know that Carlos was her brother." He looked
earnestly into my eyes.

"Half-brother," I said, automatically. Then I
amended, "They were brought up together, like
brother and sister. In New York. I met Sive."

"Yes," he said.

I wanted to tell him that I knew about Carlos, that Carlos was his son. His and Georgie's. I wanted to tell him that, but there was some impenetrable coldness in those cavernous eyes that kept me from it.

"Have you met Kathleen?" he asked.

I said, ironically, that I had had that pleasure.

"And Rollie," he added, glancing at the wound Rollie's gun barrel had inflicted. I wondered how much Jardin knew. Everything, I decided.

"According to Clara, Maria is just afraid of men," I said. "Clara says Maria was afraid of Rollie, too, and Tony even."

"Well," said Robert mildly, "maybe Maria just had bad luck with her brothers. Her husbands all have treated her well." He seemed amused again.

I wanted to sympathize with him, I wanted him to stop pretending he didn't know that Carlos was his son. I also wanted to know more about Maria's confession that she had killed Carlos. I said, "Did you ever ask Maria about that night? I mean, how did she kill him?"

Robert waved his hand. It held the check like a semaphore. I wondered what he was signaling.

"It was her fear of violence, don't you think? Carlos could be like an avenging angel. He had decided they were running drugs through Monte Cassino and he intended to get to the bottom of it. Maria was the only person he found on the island. He followed her down to that octagon on the shore . . ."

"Immaculate Conception."

"Yes." He smiled. "Immaculate Conception. She

149

climbed up into the loft. He followed her. She swung a chair at him and he lost his balance. Broke his neck apparently."

"It was an accident?"

Robert shrugged. He pulled back the wrist of his raveled cardigan to look at the time. "I must be getting back."

He dropped me at my car. He said, "I probably won't see you again before you leave. Have a good trip."

I thanked him and said I'd do my best to. His parting words were, "Give Kathleen a call before you leave."

Before I could ask him why, he darted across the street between two lines of traffic. Kathleen's house was only a few miles down the road and it was early still. I decided, what the hell. In the early afternoon, Rollie wouldn't be there. Who knows, she might even be sober.

She wasn't sober, but she was lucid. Sort of lucid. She was entertaining the television, talking to it anyway. The set, like some phosphorescent fungus, glowed dimly in the dark interior of the house. I could see its greenish aura from the kitchen door. I couldn't see Kathleen but I could hear her. She seemed to be telling her troubles to the set, already burdened with woes of its own.

Kathleen was glad to see me. "What'll you have?" she asked, then remembered. "Oh, you're the one doesn't drink. That's okay. I'll finish what you leave, and who knows, you might change your mind."

Someone had been at work on the dishes. The pile of unwashed plates and glasses had dwindled.

Kathleen took down a glass from the cupboard. "What'll it be? Vodka? Or vodka?" "Vodka'll be fine," I said. Kathleen thought that was very funny. We agreed to sit at the table in the kitchen. I hoped the television wouldn't feel lonely. The conversation at first was desultory. Kathleen mostly continuing the one she had been having with the television when I arrived, I wondering what I should say, wondering why Robert had sent me.

"Sunabitch, you think he'd tell me where he's goin'?" said Kathleen, not so much to me as to the world. I had heard her ask the very same question to the television set.

"Kathleen, do you think Maria was afraid of Carlos?" I asked.

"Sunabitch!" she said.

For ten minutes it was like some mad Menotti trio — Kathleen, me and the TV, which periodically screamed, sobbed and shot off guns in the living room. Then I stumbled onto the right question. I said wasn't it too bad about Robert Jardin, losing a son like that, and him not even knowing he had a son until after Carlos was dead.

"Robert Jardin?" said Kathleen. "I didn't know he was married."

It seemed a non sequitur. "Well," I said, "I don't think he is."

"You just said he had a son."

"Carlos."

"Carlos?" She started to say more, then checked herself.

I said, "Carlos was Jardin's son. Wasn't he?" I didn't think I could possibly be wrong. I remembered how blank Dito had looked when I mentioned Bonifacio's name to him at dinner. "You and Georgie both had babies that time you went to New York. Didn't you? You had Maria, Georgie had Carlos? You told me that."

When I mentioned Georgie's name, a net of lines formed at her eyes spilling worry like an overfull seine. Worry spilled into her voice which wavered as she said, "I never told you nothing."

I bullied. "Sure you did. You and Georgie. That time they said Georgie went abroad. You two came to New York. That's where Maria was born. Carlos too. But Bonifacio wasn't Carlos's mother. Georgie was."

"You gotta big imagination," said Kathleen. "A big imagination." She picked up "my" vodka. The table got some of it, her hand was shaking that badly.

"What's wrong, Kathleen?" I asked.

She downed the drink, and wiped her mouth with the back of her hand. She took a determined breath, and fixed her eyes wide on mine. If she didn't blink what she had to say would be true. I'd done the same myself, many times. Drunk. Sober, I'd come to realize what was true was true and my eyes had nothing to do with it.

Her elaborate preparations completed, Kathleen said, steadily and wide-eyed, "Dito is not Carlos's father."

Her brow cleared briefly, then worry gathered again in her eyes. "That's the truth so help me God. And Georgie went to Europe. I never said Georgie was anybody's mother. Did I?"

She wasn't looking me in the eye, so what she

152

just had said couldn't be trusted. That was understood. She said, "For God's sake, have a drink and let's talk about something else. You and that Jardin creep, all you wanna do is talk about Carlos. Carlos! Carlos! I hate Carlos. Have a drink, for Christ's sake."

It was funny, I thought later, driving back to Surry. Kathleen got herself all revved up to tell me a big lie, soul-baring stare and all, and then she comes up with the truth: Dito wasn't Carlos's father. Well, I knew that. Robert Jardin was. Had to have been. I went over it all again. First, it was Georgie who had given birth to Carlos, not Bonifacio. Then, that whole summer when I had watched those beautiful siblings, Georgie and Dito, at play, the only other person they ever saw was Robert Jardin. My mind filled with the images of my pubescent romancing. The gilded couple, Georgie, and her handsome brother Dito; then later, toward the end of summer, the insignificant Bobby Jardin. I could see Dito and Georgie together playing croquet, sunbathing, dancing. Those two, their beautiful young bodies swaying up and down the terrace to the beat of the tango. Dito bending his sister double under him. Brigid, hot with excitement, watching from a hundred yards away, breathing with Dito over that beloved face. Suddenly I understood. It wasn't Robert Jardin who had fathered Carlos. It was Georgie's brother Dito!

Now, there was a scandal, I thought. Even I felt breathless, the realization having hit me like a blow in the chest.

I wondered whether Kathleen had given the secret away to Robert when he called. Given it away

153

as she just had to me, under the elaborate cover of truth-telling.

I needed to talk with someone. I decided to ask Pat if she would come to dinner with me. I wished there were some way I could get rid of Barney, permanently. The open sundews of the cedar bog flashed yellow in my mind. I laughed, perhaps a little hysterically.

Chapter 11

I had three days before my week of training was to begin. Three days to clear up loose ends, and to buy myself some threads. Bruce's phrase. I checked in at the Spring Fountain Motel on the outskirts of Bucksport, then headed back toward Surry and an early supper at Duffy's. The wind had come up and there was a feel of snow in the air. At the restaurant, struggling to shut the door behind me, I heard someone call my name.

"Brigid! Son of a gun!"

It was Alex Adler, with Maria. They hadn't ordered yet and asked me to join them. It was their last night in the area — the next day they were setting out to Arizona for the winter.

"A fat farm. Owned by one of Maria's former husbands," Alex explained. "Maria cooks. I make beds. I hear you're going someplace warm, too."

"Yeah," I started to say in a matter-of-fact sort of way, then remembered that the information was still a state secret. I ended on a quavering note of question. Tried again, "Who told you that?"

"Barney," the two of them said together. Alex continued, "Said you were gallivanting off to Panama again. Well, aren't you?"

The waitress arrived just then, plates lining her arm clear up to her chin. Gave me time to adjust my face for the lie. Remembering Kathleen, I avoided their eyes and buttered my bread as I said, "First I heard of it."

"Oh right," Alex said, "Barney told us not to tell anyone." She laughed. "Barney said you're going for the DEA, like an agent."

The idea seemed to tickle her and that annoyed me. I remembered what Jardin had said about Sr. Anne taking the Guatemalan family off Monte Cassino the night of the storm. I said, "Whatever happened to Sr. Anne?"

"*Sister* Anne?" asked Alex.

Sr. Anne, it turned out, wasn't a Sister. With a leitmotif of ribald comments, Alex explained that Anne had replaced her, Alex, in Santa Clara's affections. "But not for long," she said with some satisfaction. Gesturing with her beer, she said, "Our friend Maria here soon replaced Anne. Didn't you, honey."

Maria seemed embarrassed. She said, "Last I heard from Anne she was with Covenant House in New York."

"Stop by the cabin after," said Alex. "Maria has her phone number."

Their story of the storm was different from the story Robert Jardin had told. According to them, Maria and Anne had left Monte Cassino together with the refugees. When I tried to question them further, Maria suggested that we wait until later to talk about it. She invited me to their cabin for coffee.

Their cabin looked deserted, like a waiting room after the train pulls out. Disconsolate scraps of litter lay abandoned here and there on the floor and counter tops. Maria stood in the doorway surveying the scene. When she spoke, she seemed more resigned than angry. "Alex!" she said, "you promised to sweep."

Alex, already opening a beer from the row of bottles standing on the window ledge keeping cool, laughed. "This afternoon I heard them say on the radio how they planned to have another day tomorrow."

"Bullshit!" said Maria. "We're supposed to leave in the morning at five."

"Oh, I forgot to say," returned Alex, "they plan to have another day after that."

Maria teetered on whether to let Alex have it right then or wait until I left. I said, "Hey, maybe this isn't a good time."

"Oh, have a beer," said Alex. "She'll get over it."

"Alex! You know Brigid doesn't drink."

I wanted to say not to worry, that whatever Alex was offering would be all right with me.

While Maria and I sat with our coffee, Alex began pushing a broom around. Maria had handed it to her saying just one word, "Now." When Alex in the other room began to sing the California drinking song, I confided to Maria what Jardin had told me. "He said you came in alone that night. That Anne came with the refugees later. He said . . ."

She silenced me with her eyes as mournful, suddenly, as a blood-hound's. She shook her head warningly.

The sound of Alex's solitary good fellowship abruptly ended. "What's this bullshit she's telling you, Maria?"

Alex appeared in the doorway, the broom held like a cudgel. "What's with you, woman?" she asked, shaking it at me. "You got no business coming here stirring up trouble."

Maria buried her face in her hands as if she had sought refuge there often, perhaps too often. Alex continued to rant. She suggested if I wanted to find a liar I should talk to Santa Clara. "Ask her where she was during the storm. I'll tell you where she was. She was on the island. That's where. Call Anne. She'll tell you."

Maria rose and went to her. With her eyes, Maria sent me a mute appeal. I rose to leave. "Alex," I said, "you seem to have a lot invested in believing Clara is mixed up in this."

"Invested!" Alex scoffed. Dragging Maria along behind her, she herded me toward the door. "Maybe you're right," she said. "I got twenty years invested." As I edged out into the night, she added, "Off and on."

I, of course, knew the truth: Clara was innocent; Maria wasn't. Alex's vehemence was her only defense against the fact of Maria's guilt. What was it then, that was driving me to visit Monte Cassino one last time? This question, I sensed, was multiple choice:

1. I wanted to cross-examine Clara, settle once and for all whether she had been at Monte Cassino during the blizzard, find out what, if anything, she knew about the disposal of Carlos's body.

2. I wanted to clear Clara's name of the imputation that she picked up lovers as casually as dogs pick up fleas.

3. I wanted to find out whether Clara would pick up this flea even for one night.

The answer was not to be found upside down at the bottom of my day. When I got to the spit the tide was in. It was dark. It was also windy and cold and had begun to snow, big wet flakes. I pulled the boat across to me then rowed over to the island. I didn't have a flashlight, so it was slow going up the rutted road to the community.

A welcoming light glowed dimly from the window at Clara's end of the barn. Peering in through the splashings of snow and mud, I saw her hunched disconsolately at the stove. My heart wondered how I could console her. My head told me to turn around and leave. Heart won. I tapped at the door.

"Brigid!" she said, her voice warm with surprise and welcome.

She put some sticks of wood in the stove. She gave me a cup of tea. I told her I didn't need any toast, that I had just eaten. She asked when I was leaving for Panama. I asked who had told her I was going. She wasn't sure where she'd heard it first. She thought maybe Barney.

"Terrific!" I said.

She offered to put me up for the night. In her bed. Her bed was all of two feet across. I would have accepted, but then she said she would sleep with Katie. That's the cow. Katie and Clara have a duplex. I could hear Katie next door, chewing her cud, or whatever that noise is cows make after dark.

Over tea I recited Robert Jardin's story of Maria's coming home alone, crying and out of control, the night the storm began. I admitted confronting Maria with the story. "Alex overheard," I said. "She practically threw me out." Perhaps I was looking for sympathy.

"Poor Alex," said Clara, predictably, and without any discernible emotion.

I remembered with a pang that she and Alex once were lovers.

We sat on folding chairs side by side facing the stove. Her sleeve brushed mine when she moved, when she breathed. Her knee touched my thigh. My face, my hands, my shins grew hot from the heat of the stove, my groin with another heat. I reached for her hand. She surrendered it, but let it lie flaccid in mine, uninterested, and uninteresting. It was I who broke the silence.

"Alex has it in for you, doesn't she?"

"Poor Alex," she breathed again. It felt almost as if her hand in mine had stirred.

"She says you were here the weekend of that blizzard."

Clara sighed. Her hand moved in mine, clenched slightly, as if in time she might respond to my courting fingers. I turned up her palm, began to caress the vulnerable pulse of her wrist. Again she sighed.

I said, my voice husky as an adolescent's, "Alex thinks you had Rollie get rid of the body. I mean Carlos's body."

In my ear she whispered, "Poor Alex." I could feel her breath enter hot in my ear, spread hot across my belly.

"Is it true?" I asked.

She said, "It's late and it's snowing. Won't you spend the night?"

She had turned to face me. I kept my eyes fixed on the glowing fire visible through the window in the door of the stove. I said, "I've got to be getting back."

Her finger hooked over and began to caress the hand caressing hers.

Some primitive instinct for self preservation surfaced. I stood. I thanked her for her offer. I picked my coat off the bed where she had thrown it, and putting it on I said, "Thank you, Clara, I really wish I could. Do you have a flashlight I could borrow?"

She asked how she would get it back, and I said not to bother, maybe the moon would be out, and anyway I saw pretty good in the dark. I left babbling, the tide of words carrying me out the door and far enough down the road so that momentum kept me going to the boat and on across to the mainland and my car.

Burt Reynolds was recovering from a hangover

when I got to the motel. I saw him through his ordeal, then turned off the TV set and the lights. It seemed I never slept that night, but suddenly it was day. What I was aware of all night long was Clara. Aware too of the suspicions concerning her, the suspicions held by Pat and by Alex, suspicions that Jardin seemed to have laid to rest. Had laid to rest.

I still believed in Clara's innocence. In fact I thought it somewhat noble, her cooperating with Jardin and the CIA when to do that made her vulnerable to gossip. Made her vulnerable to Sr. Barnabas's attempts at blackmail. I did wonder where the money came from that was pouring into Monte Cassino. Then I remembered how lavishly Bruce McAntee had provided for my trip to Panama, and for what. For pillow talk. I wondered what he had up his sleeve sending me to Panama again. I wondered what my training would consist of. I planned my Paitilla wardrobe. And then I reviewed the history of my strange relationship with Clara, and decided again that she was innocent and even somewhat noble to cooperate with Jardin and the CIA . . . Round and round, all night long.

Then it was day and the phone was ringing. Alex. She said, "After you left last night, Maria put her stuff in the car and took off. I'm at the convent."

"Convent?" I repeated stupidly.

"Yeah, they put me up for the night. Pat said I could stay for the winter, help put up a new barn. Might as well, no place else to go. Hey, I feel like shit."

If I didn't know better I would have thought the wrench in my gut was jealousy. Alex wintering at the convent. Alex sleeping next door to Pat. Alex hearing Pat sigh in the night through the thin pine boarding separating their beds. I decided to take a shower.

I called Bruce. He was very angry.

"I thought I told you not to tell anyone you were going to Panama. Not until I gave you the go ahead."

"I only told —"

"Half the world apparently!"

I had told only Pat. But she obviously had told Barney. It was Barney who had told half the world. Not me. I didn't try to explain this distinction to Bruce.

He told me to be at Cape Elizabeth by nine the next morning. He suggested that I not tell anyone where I would be. "Unless, of course, you already have?"

"No," I lied. "Of course I haven't."

The training, which was to have taken only a week, stretched on until after Thanksgiving. There were a lot of reasons. For one thing, Bruce said it would take more than a week to bring my Spanish back up to scratch. Then it rained. They wanted to teach me how to spot a tail and to shake one. But it was impossible to work the streets in the rain, which on many days was torrential, like a tropical downpour except for being so cold. Bruce said he saw no reason for me to learn self-defense, but I told him I'd just as soon. The days it rained I spent working out in the gym in the basement of the

163

house where I stayed and where the rest of the training occurred. Bruce said after a week that as a student "I'd do." He said, "You start doing what you're told and you might even survive." Then he added, "Only joking." I said, "Some joke."

They let me out at night. That's when I bought my threads. Bruce said to get a decent suitcase. "In fact, get two."

Thanksgiving was turkey with all the trimmings. I'd never had Thanksgiving with G-men before. We had it in Spanish. That part I liked. I had begun to think in Spanish, and Bruce said I was set to go. I left that Friday for Panama.

I spent the night at the Paitilla Holiday Inn, in a room with a view across the bay toward San Felipe and the Presidential Palace. Susan and her husband Frank had met me at Tocumen, Susan insisting that I return with them to Curundu. I had been tempted. It was raining cats and dogs when I arrived, the humidity palpable as warm consommé. My real linen slacks and real silk shirt were a rumpled mess. I would have felt more elegant, that first night in Paitilla, wearing my regulation jeans and T-shirt. When I explained to Susan that I didn't want to put their lives in danger, she laughed and said, "Oh, Brigid!" But she stopped urging me. Frank never had.

"Let me take you to dinner tomorrow," I suggested. "Let's go to Las Tinajas."

They agreed, finally.

No one in the lobby snickered as I registered,

maybe because everything about me was too wilted to be polyester. My room was large and generic. But the view was strictly Panama. I shoved one of the overstuffed chairs to the window and collapsed, waiting for that special feeling to come, that feeling of being home again, at last. But it didn't, and I grew restless. It was the air, I decided. The air, like the room, was generic. I wanted to breathe Panamanian air. But I didn't want to face that lobby again. My divided self debated what to do. We achieved a compromise. I would go down the stairwell and sneak out the back. Problem: could I get in again? Solution: I would cross that bridge when I came to it.

The stairwell was made for blue jeans, and I thought I might like to hang out there. Other people did, you could see their ground-out butts littering the area by the door. My room was on the sixth floor. On the landing of the fifth I heard a door above me open. I happened to be catching my breath, otherwise, singing *Panameño, Panameño* as I was, I would not have heard the door, would not have realized there was someone in the stairwell with me. Self-conscious, I stopped singing. Oddly, I heard no footsteps. Whoever it was had probably ducked out for a smoke, I thought. So, jauntily I descended another flight. Then I heard the rustle of paper as someone lightly walked on the litter of paper strewn across the fourth floor landing. That made me nervous. On the third floor I tried to exit the stairwell, but the locked door only opened inward. Then the lights went out.

I froze. The person above me continued to move slowly downstairs. "Hello!" I cried. No answer.

It was dark in the stairwell, but some light filtered in under the doors, and I could see below me the red glow of an exit sign. My hand found the iron railing and I started down, my fancy new sandals clacking noisily on the concrete, obliterating any sound my companion might have made.

In the thin line of light under the second floor door I saw the corner of a box. Groping as I passed, I caught hold of the rim. It took a precious second to wheel, grab the box and lift it. I put it down against the rail at the head of the flight of stairs, and continued my clattering descent. A moment later my friend ran into it. "*Carajo! Pendejo!*" I heard above the noises made by the box, my sandals and my beating heart. Then I was at the red exit sign and a door that would open.

Out of the frying pan into the fire. The exit was onto an alley lined with garbage cans and derelict cars, the only creatures in sight a couple of cats. I ran toward the corner. But no one followed me. Disheveled and panting, I re-entered the hotel behind a group of revelers, I hoped inconspicuously. Back in my room I checked to see whether anyone had been through my things. No one but the man at customs. I chained the door. And drew a bath. What I needed, and badly, was a soothing nightcap. I called room service. "Warm milk and honey, please — and some cinnamon toast." Big deal.

I lived through the chase a score of times during the night, waking next morning to find I had vanquished my bedclothes. The sun was shining and I felt eager as a colt to be out and running around. Fearless, I exited via the stairwell, wearing, this time, a pair of tennis shoes. The raincoat I had bought for the trip was a bright blue poncho. With it flowing behind me as I trotted down the stairs I felt like Wonder Woman. I decided what I needed was some magic bracelets and I knew just where to find them.

In front of the hotel stood a line of taxis. Looking them over, I picked one whose driver, a man perhaps my age, his hair short and grizzled like white foam on dark rock, stood at the side of his cab gazing hopefully out to sea. He was a Jamaican, it turned out, and didn't speak Spanish, except, he said, to get by with. His name was Ed. He agreed to take me shopping and sight-seeing.

Our first target was Central Avenue with all its shops. I did want to get some Wonder Woman bracelets. With poncho, bracelets and tennis shoes, I would be up to any adventure. Judiciously I decided to buy some perfume also, Joy, if I could find it, because for once I could afford it. And a hat. The CIA training had been wonderful, but none of my trainers had had a clue what it took to fortify the inner woman.

Two rain squalls punctuated our drive down Avenida Balboa. At Balboa's statue I got out and walked around just for the joy of it, for the feel of the air on my skin and the smell of it in my nose, for the medley of tongues, and to hear the sound of wind stirring palm fronds at the ocean's edge. For the feeling of being home. Thomas Wolfe was wrong. Home is where you were born, and your body knows it. Maybe, I reflected, only colonials experience this physical recognition of birthplace. We're like salmon, wandering all our lives, so when we come back our recognition is carnal, and visceral, not intellectual.

My skin knew I was home, and my gut was glad. Ed said, "You look happy, Miss."

"Yeah," I said. "Some happy."

Ed was worried about me shopping on Central Avenue. He told me things were different in Panama from when I was a girl. "Not safe," he said, "not like before." Modesty kept me from telling him what a star pupil of self-defense I had been. So, I agreed to have him come with me. I found my bracelets at Salomon's Bazaar, scrolled silver bands about an inch wide, like ones I'd had as a child. As a child, when I wore them I had been Wonder Woman too.

From Central Avenue we drove to the ruins of Old Panama, Panamá Viejo, laid waste centuries before by that pirate Henry Morgan. Bliss. Bliss to hear the music of Salsa loud from a dozen brightly painted *chiva* busses. Bliss to stroll from ruined cathedral to ruined convent. I was less aware of the people there that day, from Africa and India, Europe and Asia, than I was aware of those with whom I had come so many years before, and of those ghosts seen in family photo albums: youth in sailor suits posing in gaping ruins with laughing girls in gingham, lost uncles and aunts, mother and father.

Ed said I mustn't forget the Golden Altar, saved from Morgan and now in a small church in Chorrillo, the oldest section of Panama City. Back down Balboa Avenue we rode to the heart of the city, the old heart, the worn-out heart, the heart of poverty, the heart of hope, where the balconies of wooden tenements bloomed with flowers and with people.

It seemed to have stopped raining for the day and I decided that I would like to wander around alone for a while. I wanted to climb Ancon hill at the edge of what had once been the Canal Zone, and to look down on the city from there. I asked Ed how much I owed him and added a big tip, to show our gratitude, mine and Uncle Sam's.

He thanked me. His parting words were, "You take care, hyar. It not like it used to be. It not safe no more." Instead of returning to his cab, he ambled down the block. It must have been home. Several children greeted him and a woman his age, perhaps his wife, met him at the doorway of a stairwell leading up to the second floor tenements. Ed turned and saw me watching. The two of them waved. I felt connected.

In all this time I hadn't once checked to see whether anyone was tailing me. I was supposed to look for two kinds of tail, good guys and bad guys. Good guys not before Monday. Bad guys all the time. Good guys might want to tell me something. Bad guys I wanted to shake.

I became aware of the bad guy as I wandered across the grass at the top of Ancon hill. Actually I had been aware of him for some time walking behind me up the broad path from Avenida de los Martiers. But not until I realized we were the only two people at the summit, did it register. As I turned to go back down, I found him lounging against a wire link fence alongside the path, big, muscular and ugly.

He was smoking his cigarette in a lazy sort of way, the smoke curling slowly from his nostrils. I nodded and said, *"Buenas Tardes."* He nodded too, but was silent. He seemed amused. I turned and headed back toward the summit, uncertain what to do next. I wondered how my self-defense would work against someone less compliant than a trainer. I wondered how to get out of there without using the path. The descent down the Ancon side of the hill was too sheer to maneuver. Glancing over my shoulder, I saw him still following. Catching my eye, he smiled. He flicked his cigarette away. I watched the long slow trajectory as it sailed off into space. I turned and began to run.

It was a silly thing to do, up hill and nowhere to hide. Circling back I came upon him again, lighting another cigarette. This time he laughed. I was too out of breath to join in the joke. He gestured with his cigarette, come, come.

"*¿Qué quiere?*" I panted.

In unaccented English, he replied. "Boss wants to see you."

I said, "Terrific. I don't want to see him."

A child skipped into view. I heard someone, her father perhaps, further down the hill and out of sight, call to her. She stood for a moment looking curiously at us, and then she turned obediently and ran away.

My man stood lounging, waiting, one hand in his pocket. Condescendingly he motioned again with his cigarette for me to come. He showed me the handle of the gun he held, drawing it slowly from his pocket, a lazy gesture, obscene as flashing.

"Who's your boss?" I asked.

"You'll see," he said, and turned, waving for me to follow him.

I debated running around the summit again for exercise. I shrugged and began to walk meekly behind. We passed a couple of kids on the way down, and a lizard. No one to pass a message to or ask for help. The little girl and her father had disappeared. We ended up in the parking lot outside Quarry Heights, the car a dilapidated VW Bug. My friend with the gun in his pocket said, "Get in." I said, "No way."

It was a hot and lazy afternoon, anyone with any sense had gone indoors to stay cool, have a drink, take a nap. So quiet there in the parking lot where we stood that bees, busy on the yellow anthers of red hibiscus flowers, buzzed loud as distant traffic. A palm nut dropping on the pavement startled us both. "Get in!" he said again, caressing his arsenal.

We stood at the door of the Bug, my back to it, he crowding me, blocking my way. He had on a *guayabera*, the embroidered shirt men in Panama wear. He smelled of tobacco and a heavy perfume. Crouching, he reached behind me to ease open the door. I could feel the hard barrel of his gun jab my thigh. "Don't even think about it," he muttered, his hand closing over my mouth and nose, so that catching my breath I sucked in his odor and choked. He kneed me backwards onto the seat. He said, "You don't got a handle, so don't try to get out. You scream, you just make it harder for yourself."

I looked down and where the handle once had been there was a rusty, gaping hole. His head and shoulders blocked the window. He grinned. One of his two front teeth was missing. The other was big and ridged still like a child's. "Be good now," he said and wheeled around the hood.

He headed down toward the city, through a maze of streets lined with shops and restaurants, sidewalks crowded with tables of merchandise. Neon signs blinked bright invitations, red, green and blue, to dine, to drink, to dance. And a thousand people, indifferent to me as stars in the Milky Way, churned about, haggling, barking, buying, stealing.

As we moved east toward Paitilla, the streets grew more sober until finally we entered the sedate, tree-shaded neighborhood of luxury hotels and embassies, where high walls topped with broken glass hid mysterious interiors. Through wrought iron gates I caught sight of inviting green lawns and flowering trees, of sprawling stucco palaces. We stopped at one of these. A boy in bright white pants and shirt opened the gate.

Dito stood waiting under the portico for us. "I'm so sorry, Brigid," he said, "for any inconvenience this might have caused you."

"Jesus Christ! Dito," I said, "Inconvenience! Is that what you call being kidnapped off Ancon hill by Schwarzenegger over there, inconvenient?"

With impeccable manners Dito had moved to the door and was standing, slightly bowed, inviting me to precede him into the cool interior of his house. For the past half hour I had been imagining a Dr. Frankenstein sort of laboratory to be my destination, so it was relief that had fueled my explosion. Dito's face was as blandly understanding as a shrink's.

"Would you care for a drink?" he asked when we reached the room he had chosen for our meeting. "Sit down, sit down," he urged hospitably, and I chose a bamboo armchair looking out on an immaculate green lawn made intimate by high oleander bushes smelling sweet as honeysuckle. The room was open, a grille of wrought iron flowers in the wide windows. "If you prefer," said Dito, "we could go where there is air conditioning."

"This is fine," I said. "I don't want a drink."

"I thought maybe, under the circumstances," he laughed mildly, "you might change your mind. Tea then? Or coffee? Iced coffee."

"Water."

He snapped his fingers and for the first time I noticed a woman, not unlike the young Bonifacio, hovering in shadow by the door. She vanished to return a moment later with a tray bearing a glass of water, peanuts in a silver bowl, and an iced drink for Dito.

"You're wondering," said Dito, drawing his chair close to mine, "what this is all about."

Actually I was beyond wondering. From that first sickening moment with my captor I knew: 1) I had been set up again and there were no good guys to save me, their shift didn't start until Monday; and 2) whoever had wanted me dead wasn't going to mess around staging a phony accident this time. The only thing I wondered was what they planned to do with my body. But I tried to keep my mind away from that question.

"Brigid, Brigid," said Dito, being avuncular. "You're frightened. But you must know you have nothing to fear from me. Our mothers were best friends. My mother was your godmother. Have you forgotten that?"

I sipped my water, wishing it were whiskey, Irish whiskey, straight up. God*mother!* Big deal. Dito looked to me like a god*father*, Panama style, with a crisp white *guayabera* elaborately embroidered, white linen slacks, and open sandals, the hair on his toes shining like copper in a beam of sunlight.

"Look at me, Brigid," said Dito, and I reluctantly pulled my eyes away from their study of his toes. "I wanted to warn you."

I must have looked stony-faced, for he sighed and stood up and began to pace the floor behind me. He said I had gotten in over my head. He told me that he had decided he had no choice but to warn me. He said he had done many things in his life that he regretted, and that before he died he wanted to do one thing right. That was why, he explained, he had brought me here to his house.

"If you call having me kidnapped by Arnold Schwarzenegger something good I don't want to know about the bad stuff," I said.

They were the first words I had uttered since asking for water. Dito must have taken it for a good sign. He sat down beside me again, his knee touching mine. "You always had a marvelous sense of humor," he said enthusiastically.

I shifted, breaking contact with his knee. I had felt myself relaxing. Fearing hope like a bad omen, I tried to renew my terror, deliberately bringing to mind my accident on the road leaving El Valle. But I refused to think about that note someone had slipped into my pocket outside Bonifacio's apartment. The one threatening me with a bat.

"I'd like to go," I said.

"In a moment, if you insist. But I do want you to stay for dinner. Have a swim in the pool. It's so hot."

"I'm going to Las Tinajas with Susan and Frank," I said.

"How perfect! You shall be my guests."

"I don't think so."

"Brigid, I believe what you are doing is admirable. I have always admired Bruce. This drug business is dreadful. You know I have suffered personally. My own son. Tony."

He looked away. His gesture of suppressing sorrow I thought was theatrical. But then I heard his breathing change and realized he was struggling to keep from sobbing.

"You never knew Tony before," he said finally. "Before the drugs."

In spite of myself I felt sorry for him.

"Bruce is using you," said Dito. "Everyone in this business is ruthless. I don't think you realize. So much at stake." His gesture included, I guess, his pool, his Cadillacs, his servants, his manicured lawns. He buried his well-groomed head in his hands. "Spadaforo," he groaned.

"Spadaforo?" I repeated, curious and frightened. "Hugo Spadaforo?" A one-time friend of Noriega's, Spadaforo's body minus the head had turned up in the interior a few years before. According to the papers he and Noriega had had a falling out. "What about Spadaforo?"

Dito raised his head. He looked like a creature of Michelangelo's contemplating hell. "He was a friend. A good friend."

I said, inadequately, "Too bad."

Our roles seemed slowly to have reversed. I had become the comforter, Dito the one needing comfort. I said, "I guess you don't want to mess around with that crackpot Noriega."

"Noriega? Oh!" he exclaimed scornfully. "Noriega!

Your *New York Times* says Noriega this, Noriega that."

"Noriega didn't have Spadaforo killed?"

"What for? They were friends! The Big Lie. You never heard about the Big Lie? Your country is the Big Lie."

"My country? Come off it, Dito."

He rose and went to the archway entrance to the hall and clapped. The Bonifacio-like woman emerged from the shadow. He spoke to her in rapid Spanish and she disappeared. When he returned he had regained his composure.

"You are right, Brigid. We both are children of the Big Lie. *La mentira.* Do you remember your Spanish?"

"A little," I said.

"Good. You may need it."

"Meaning?"

"Why do you think Bruce asked you to come back to Panama?"

"He wants to uncover whoever is directing the distribution of drugs in Maine."

"So he sends you *here*," said Dito sarcastically.

"Yes," I said defensively. "He's having certain people watched, in Maine. See who gets in touch with you, for instance. And Georgie." Whistling in the dark, I added, "They know I'm here."

He chuckled, avuncular again, and fond. "Little Brigid," he said. "Never mind. You have someone to watch over you." He tapped his broad, barrel chest. *"Moi!"* He said, "But after tonight, after our dinner at Las Tinajas, I want you to return to Maine. I have made reservations for you on Monday's flight. You'll stay here until then. I have arranged for your belongings to be brought from the hotel. Here you will be safe until Monday."

"Nonsense! I'll do no such thing."

"Well, talk with Frank and Susan. See what they advise. They'll be here in a while. I have sent a car to bring them."

Just like that! I remembered the last time Dito and I had met, in Maine at the funeral of his son Tony. How he had ordered Robert Jardin around: "Pay the check! Go get the car!" And how meekly Robert had obeyed. At least until the subject of Carlos had come up and Robert had defected, leaving me to play chauffeur for a night. I thought how Dito had used Robert over the years, from that summer when he and Georgie began to include him in their games — had they considered having Georgie marry him? — to the present and Robert's apparent willingness to play *consigliere* to Dito's godfather. How, I wondered, did Robert Jardin take it? Dito's maddening assumption of authority over everyone around him made me want to break up the furniture, but I managed to restrain myself.

After some polite-host chit-chat and a tour of the grounds, Dito summoned "Bonifacio" to show me to my room. He said he hoped it would please me, but if it didn't, I could choose another. Perhaps I would prefer air conditioning, for instance.

Sour, chafed by the bridle of Dito's calm self-assurance, and goaded by my own feeling of helplessness, I growled, "Yeah, I'll do that."

The room was lovely, shaded by an avocado tree and perfumed with coral vine. At the end of a long corridor, it opened onto a small private garden. My bags had been unpacked. "Bonifacio" asked what she could bring to make me comfortable. I said, *"Nada. Gracias."* Dito had said that Frank and Susan would arrive at 7:00 p.m. for drinks before dinner. It was only a little after 5:00 p.m. My dinner time in Maine. I was starving.

I took a cold shower, donned a cotton wrap I found in the bath and went outside to sit and think things over. On the table by the chaise lounge I found a covered dish with cheeses and bread and beside it a glass of freshly squeezed orange juice. The glass of juice reminded me of Georgie. Georgie reminded me of things I didn't want to remember. I suddenly wasn't hungry any more.

On our tour of his grounds, Dito had confided to me, with the manner of a doctor confiding disturbing details to the next-of-kin, what he referred to as "some unpleasant facts." He said that Noriega had been the darling of our CIA until Panama hosted the Contadora meetings to bring the wars in Central America to an end. Only after Noriega had refused any longer to help arm the Contra mercenaries in Honduras had Noriega been cut out of the floating crap game staked by the drugs-for-arms trade and protected by the CIA. Near tears again, Dito alluded to Spadaforo's decapitation, to his son Tony's addiction and death by overdose — overdose or adulterated drugs that had poisoned him.

Strolling among his prize roses, admiring the orchids hanging from the boughs of the jacaranda tree, I had nearly fallen for his line. I'd heard the charges before, of course. But there was something about Dito's complacent assumption of virtue that curdled my conviction and left me unsettled. Left me, finally, unconvinced. It was all to convenient, his kidnapping me and then pacifying me with his Looking-Glass version of things. Robert Jardin, working for the CIA, and his ally Bruce McAntee — they weren't my friends. No! Dito Brown was my friend. After all, wasn't his mother my godmother? Trust him!

Trust him until when? Monday when my absence was noted by Bruce's men? Or trust him until later in the week when I would have been given up for lost — and then what? Would it be my head they discovered in some remote province? Or would it be my decapitated body? I carefully kept my mind away from what condition my body, if it were found, might be in.

In short I spent an hour terrifying myself in Dito's gentle garden. An hour building up my determination to get out of his soft prison. An hour being a little crazy before I went indoors and got dressed for dinner.

Las Tinajas was lovely, had I only been able to enjoy it. My companions seemed to have a good time. They certainly were feeling no pain. Frank and Susan had arrived at the house promptly at 7:00 p.m. We didn't get to Las Tinajas until after nine and the two of them and Dito were already well oiled when we got there. Dito had reserved a table at the edge of the dance floor. The dancers were performing when we arrived, three beautiful women in *Polleras,* their heads shining with the bobbing beads of their *timbleques,* three men in *Montunos,* the men seductive, the women alluring, the music exciting, and I wished I were dancing too.

Dancing, dipping my head to the open flower of Clara's ear, as the men circling the swaying women dipped theirs. One woman reminded me of Georgie, the Georgie of my adolescent fantasies. Her smooth round shoulders gyrated seductively, drawing her man slowly after her as she circled the floor. Drew me slowly after her. After Georgie, after Clara. After a longing that filled my body, or emptied it. A leaning tower of yearning.

I was returned to reality abruptly. Leaning forward, leaning halfway across our table toward the dancing woman, I had knocked over Susan's drink. It splashed in a gay little waterfall into her lap. She shrieked. Dito laughed. Georgie/Clara smiled, and so did her man. I said, "Shit!"

Susan said, "Brigid, look what you've done!"

Dito rose, pulled back Susan's chair, and said to me, "Brigid, take her to the Ladies Room." So, of course, I did.

Coming out of the rest room, Susan's dress and spirits more or less restored, I saw Robert Jardin. He was standing at the door of the restaurant. He must have been looking for me, he seemed so relieved when he caught sight of us. He beckoned.

Joy, like dawn breaking, slowly rose inside me, all the chimeras that fear had engendered dissolving in its light. For the first time since noon and my encounter with Schwarzenegger on Ancon Hill I felt my own person. I pulled Susan, protesting, behind me to the door, to Robert, to safety.

"Brigid, thank God you're okay," he said, relief

shining in the deep wells of his eyes. "Susan, Robert Jardin. We've met."

"I know that!" she said, indignant and a little drunk.

"This way," said Jardin, urgently, pulling me by the arm.

"Come on, Brigid," said Susan, pulling my other arm.

Suddenly two men appeared forming with Robert a movable wall around Susan and me; they carried us through the door and out into the tropical night. A black stretch limousine waited at the curb. Susan and I were lifted and deposited inside it, Susan with two men, one on either side of her, facing backwards and I, across from her, our knees touching, Robert on one side of me, a stranger on the other. The man on Susan's left rapped the glass partition behind him. The car started smoothly away from the curb, away from Las Tinajas and Dito Brown. But somehow I no longer felt as safe as when I first caught sight of Robert Jardin in the doorway of Las Tinajas and he beckoned for me to come to him.

I asked, "Robert, where are we going?"

He didn't answer. The jacket of the man opposite me had fallen open. His pocket, just like Schwarzeneggers's, bulged. For the first time I looked into his face. He was studying mine with cool amusement. It was my old friend, Schwarzenegger himself.

"Oh shit!" I said.

Chapter 12

We seemed to be on our way to the interior, crossing the Bridge of the Americas and heading west toward Chorrera, El Valle, Costa Rica. "Where're you taking us?" I asked.

Robert nodded to Schwarzenegger who unfolded two cotton sacks. They each contained a gag. He gagged me first, then slipped a sack over my head and tied it. Hardly able to breathe, I reached up and tried to remove the rough burlap. It was dusty and foul smelling, and I had started to sneeze. My pal Arnold grabbed my hands and roughly tied my wrists behind me. Susan started to cry out. Whoever hit her, hit hard. Twice. One blow was a slap, the other knocked the wind out of her. I heard her gasp for breath until that sound too was cut off by the gag.

The thought of my own decapitation had terrified me, but the sound of my baby cousin Susan being brutalized enraged me. I remembered teaching her, in El Valle, how to ride bareback, and that memorable time, when we were walking in the bush and she had had to wipe her butt, how I had advised her to use leaves but hadn't mentioned to watch out for the local variant of poison ivy. I could see her as she had been on her first date with Bruce McAntee, how gorgeous they had looked together in the prom photo, slim and athletic, her hair a bright red tangle of curls, his sandy hair leveled in a flat-top that hid his cowlick, both so freckled and all-American, or our colonial version of that quality.

I yearned toward her silence and thought of Frank. Poor Frank! I remembered their wedding, how his dark good looks had seemed designed to foil her Irish beauty. How well his even temperament supported her Irish volatility. Frank would kill me for getting her into this mess. Yeah! Right. Provided we lived that long.

The trip seemed to take several days, as if we had gone to Costa Rica at least. They stopped more than once, at taverns it sounded like. The windows had shades, and these they pulled before we stopped. A day or two into our journey, Robert anticipated my need. He said, "You ladies want to use a rest room?" He said where we were was miles away from civilization, that it wouldn't do us any good to make a ruckus. He said if we tried anything we would pay for it. "Pay dearly," he said.

I never saw where it was. But it couldn't have been civilized — they didn't take off my gunny sack. It had slowly become clear to me that Robert never intended to let us go. Kidnapping us from Las Tinajas wasn't something he would be able to explain away. I wondered whether my chum Bruce McAntee was in on this caper. Sometimes I decided he had to be; other times I wasn't so sure. I wondered how much Clara knew.

When I thought Bruce was innocent, I thought so because of how lavishly he had bankrolled my two trips to Panama. I reasoned that it had to have been government money he was spending.

But if Bruce was a government man, so was Robert Jardin. Bruce had said so. And if Jardin was CIA, Clara's alliance with him was harmless. If Bruce was innocent, ipso facto, so was Clara. I liked that. My problem was it didn't compute. The burlap sack over my head made nonsense of any logic that demonstrated Jardin's innocence.

Then I'd start to thinking about how much money there is in drugs. A cartel's bankroll probably seems as bottomless as the U.S. Treasury. If Bruce and Jardin were kingpins of the drug setup in Maine, they would have tried to convince me they were government men, CIA and CENTAC.

And where would that leave Clara? Up to her ears in shit, that's where.

I tried to cut it differently, to separate Jardin from Bruce and Clara. Say Bruce was on the level, Clara too, and Jardin *was* with the CIA. Jardin still could be directing the flow of drugs into the States through Canada. Maybe Dito had been telling the truth after all. Whatever else, this version allowed for Clara and Bruce both to be innocent. And if they were innocent, Brigid Donovan wasn't quite so big a shmuck as she otherwise would seem to be. The comfort I derived from this solution made me distrust it.

Somewhere along the way, like Guatemala, I had another thought that was reassuring. If Dito had been telling the truth, then he knew what he was talking about. That meant he would have a good idea where Jardin planned to take us. I let my mind wander down these hopeful corridors a while.

My hopes centered on Dito's defense of Noriega. Spadaforo, Dito had said, was Noriega's friend. Dito had been Spadaforo's friend. Dito, therefore, must be a friend of Noriega's. And Noriega had at his command several thousand loyal troops called the Dignity Battalions, which were stationed all over the country. I liked the scene in my mental drama where I, all unmindful of their threats, was hurling defiance at Schwarzenegger and Jardin when suddenly the door to the dungeon flew open and there on the threshold stood a wedge of combat troops, their Uzis ready to blow my tormenters away.

In all those dreadful, uncomfortable hours of the trip, I hadn't once thought of Georgie.

I found out later that our endless drive had taken only three hours. It was still dark when Susan and I were pulled from the car and frog-marched over grass and then down stone steps into a damp room smelling of earth and mold. The light, when they removed the burlap sack, was harsh and it took a moment for my eyes to adjust.

When I could open them, my eyes were drawn to a curious medley of sounds — scratching, rustling and high pitched squeaks. There on a hospital gurney stood a cage full of bats, small and furry and frantic to escape. At the same instant I detected the smell of Joy Parfum.

"Brigid, kitten, see what curiosity has done to you?" Georgie entered the cellar looking genuinely unhappy.

"Fuck you," I said.

She shook her head sadly. "Susan. You too. Such a shame to involve you in this mess."

Susan, who had recovered her consciousness as well as her temper, retorted, "You're in deep shit, Georgie."

Georgie laughed.

"Cut the crap!" said Jardin.

Georgie's eyebrows lifted slightly in moderate surprise, but whether at Jardin's language or his assertiveness wasn't clear.

"Georgie," said Jardin, "I'll take care of this. You go back upstairs."

"My, my," said Georgie, now mildly amused.

Jardin didn't notice. Fatuous as a bridegroom he strutted. Proud like a bantam cock. He waved a heavy black revolver, substitute for wattles and comb, threateningly at Susan and me. He said again, "I'll take care of these two. Go on upstairs, dearest. I have everything under control."

Georgie's laugh was mocking. She said, "Robert, please don't be tiresome."

Jardin was facing me when Georgie laughed, an arch tinkle of sound, a cocktail-party sort of put-down. The gun in his hand steadied. I watched his expression harden, the pride and authority displaced by a bad-boy bravado. Over his shoulder I could see Georgie's face. It belied the merriment in her voice. She was watching Jardin carefully. I was afraid she had gone too far. So was she.

A sudden pounding on the door interrupted this battle of wills between them. *"¡Entre!"* Jardin and Georgie called simultaneously. The door opened and a young Indian, his hair long like the man who had driven me off the valley road, entered. He carried a package wrapped in brown paper, *"Lo tengo,"* he said. I have it. He offered the box to Jardin.

Jardin seemed momentarily disconcerted, but he quickly recovered. He told the man to get out. Georgie at the same time said, *"¿Que tienes?"*

The man was torn. He looked from Jardin to Georgie, then wistfully at the box he held. He set the package down. Set it on the gurney next to the bats. He looked slyly at me as he pulled off the string.

Jardin lost control. *"¡Parate!"* he screamed, brandishing his gun in the Indian's face.

"I said let him open it," Georgie insisted, her voice soft and accustomed to obedience. Jardin, still wild, whipped around, his gun now under Georgie's nose. She calmly palmed it out of her face. "Sit down, Bobby," she said. "You're exhausted."

"Georgie," he whined, "You don't want to see what's in there."

She said, "Sit down."

The Indian had paused, the brown paper wrapping half off the box. Blood had seeped through the cardboard, a Rorschach stain drifting along the bottom edge.

"Oh Christ," Jardin moaned, but he went obediently to the chair and sat.

"*¡Abrelo!*" Georgie commanded tersely.

The Indian removed the lid.

Dito's face was tranquil, as apparently in command as when he had waved my attention to his palatial surroundings, reminding me how much was at stake in this game I had blundered into.

Georgie's reaction surprised me. She simply said, "My God!" in that soft voice. Susan started to gag. Looking back, I realize that I was in a state of shock, where I stayed for the next few hours.

Curtly, Georgie told the bearer of Dito's head to wrap it back up and leave. Then she said, "Robert, what did you plan to do with it?"

Jardin, looking miserable, said, "Georgie, I warned him. I told him Noriega couldn't be trusted. I reminded him of Spadaforo. I couldn't talk any sense into him."

"Ah," said Georgie. "Noriega."

"Don't believe him!" I cried.

Georgie rounded on me. For the first time since she descended the cellar stairs, she looked me in the face, let me look in hers. The merciless light of the naked bulb exposed her, exposed her years, exposed her grief, her eyes blackened with a sorrow nothing in her manner or voice had revealed.

"Be quiet, Brigid," she said. Then, still looking at

me coldly, she gave another order. "Robert, take care of these two."

"What are you going to do with us, Georgie?" I asked.

In reply she simply laughed, the sound demure, ladylike. Her eyes rested momentarily on the cage of bats. "Poor kitten," she murmured, and she started up the stairs, disappearing into the darkness of the night.

Jardin stared after her for a moment as if he still were dazed. But when he turned to face Susan and me, his air of authority had returned. "Meddlers," he muttered. "Tie them," he commanded Schwarzenegger.

"Why tie us?" I said. "We can't get out."

"Tie them," he repeated, unnecessarily. Arnold had already knocked me to the ground and had begun to string me up, my wrists lashed to my ankles behind me.

Georgie's voice suddenly boomed unnaturally loud from a speaker set on a rafter of the ceiling. "Robert, just have the door guarded. Don't tie them. They can't do much harm in the half hour they have left."

Schwarzenegger continued to do his Boy Scout routine on my arms and legs, pulling the rope until I cried out, and then jerking it one more time for good measure.

"You heard her," said Jardin. "Out!"

I couldn't see, my face pressed against the hard packed dirt of the floor. But I heard Susan yell, "Get outta here you big ape, didn't you hear your boss? Get outta here!"

189

Jardin repeated, "I said out! Just guard the door."

A moment later Susan began to worry the knot at my wrist. "Turn me over, Susan," I managed to utter.

"Ooops," she said. "Sorry."

Susan struggled with my bonds in silence, and I, silent too, took stock of our situation, calculating our chances of survival. They seemed slight. Georgie's total ruthlessness, despite my previous experience, had astonished me. As for Jardin the Wimp, what amazed me about him was that after all that had happened, despite a lifetime of subservience and betrayal, he was obviously still addicted to Georgie. He probably called it love, I reflected. Killing Dito seemed to have forged for Jardin a little of the stuff of independence but only, it seemed, when Georgie wasn't around to forbid it.

"We gotta get outta here!" Susan hissed in my ear.

"Yeah. How?"

"I got an idea."

Susan's "ideas" were notorious, like swapping the furniture in our parents' homes to get their reaction, she had explained. I didn't like this new idea of hers much, either, but I couldn't think of a better one. I figured the worst that could happen was that Schwarzenegger would forget his orders and we'd die fifteen minutes ahead of schedule. St. Peter probably wouldn't mind. And for us there would be this advantage: our death would be quicker, easier, and our own adrenalin would act like a sedative so we'd feel no pain. Or so I had heard.

We pushed the gurney over to the door. Susan gave me a surgical knife which she found in a steel sterilizer. She armed herself with a crowbar. Then we got on the gurney, one on either side of the bat cage.

Swallowing my revulsion, I hovered beside the cage, trying to keep my hand from shaking, biting my lips so that I wouldn't scream every time I felt their wings, or their mouths, brush my hand. Then Susan started to pound on the door and yell, "Fire! Fire! Let us out!"

Schwarzenegger's voice, loud and menacing, boomed, "Fuck off you two and shut up!"

Weakly, Susan said, "Well, it's true."

Arnold's reply was a loud thump on the door.

"¡Pendejo!" said Susan sullenly.

Just then we heard Jardin shout, "Bring those two up here."

Susan and I exchanged a doubtful look. "Let's go for it," Susan said and raised the crowbar over her shoulder ready to swing.

"Don't you two nuts try nothin' when I open this door," Schwarzie warned, "or you're meat."

Susan nodded and winked. It was easy for her to wink, the crucial part of our plan depended on me.

As it turned out, my timing was perfect. As Ugly eased open the door, his gun ready to fire, I eased open the door of the cage and the squealing bats swooped into his face. Susan cracked him good with the crowbar and we were out and running down the road.

It was still dark and probably would be for another hour. The moon had set, but the sky was

191

bright with stars and some of that light reflecting off the road made it possible, once our eyes became accustomed, to see where we were going.

"We gotta get off this road," said Susan.

"How?" I asked.

"Follow me," she said.

She pulled me into the brush. Just in time. A car from above us, from Georgie's, pulled slowly onto the road, its headlights illuminating the dirt like a stage.

The car passed close enough to us so that we could see Jardin was driving. Georgie, on the passenger side, seemed to look straight into my eyes as they passed. A few hundred yards further, Georgie began to search the brush on either side of the road with a flashlight, the kind you use for jacking deer.

"That was lucky," whispered Susan.

"Yeah," I whispered back. "Do you know how to get us out of here?"

"Somewhere around here there's a path."

"Going where?"

"Over to the falls."

The only falls I knew of were across the valley. "Why do we want to go to the falls?" I asked.

Nerves had made her testy. "God, Brigid, you know as well as I do there's a path out of the valley from there."

I thought about it. I could see we didn't want to be parading around in the open. But circling the valley on jungle paths just to hit the road again, even outside the valley, seemed a great deal of effort for very little gain.

"Then what?" I asked.

"Oh shut up!" she said.

The going was hard all the way, but the first two hours, those hours just before dawn, were hell. Only terror kept us moving. Terror of the human predators we had for the moment escaped and terror of the jungle predators whose presence we sensed all around us.

We had to feel our way through the jungle. It was too dark to see the path, too dark to see what our feet would trod on next. With each step we imagined the coral snake asleep on the path, the cat crouched on a branch overhead. The strap of Susan's flimsy sandal broke after about five minutes and she had to go on barefooted. I offered to share my sandals with her. She said no thanks, that she'd rather step on something nasty than break her ankle. She had a point. I took off my sandals too. For the most part the path was packed dirt and, except for our imaginings, not unpleasant to walk on.

After a time we came to the falls where the streams that circle the valley meet. The darkness had thinned and we could almost see. We bathed our feet awhile in the cold pool that formed beneath the falling water. Susan had cut her toe. The bleeding had stopped, but it looked raw and painful. She made light of it, but I, knowing how quickly infections begin and spread in the tropics, was worried. I thought I could already see a faint red line.

"Hey," she said, "I'll take an infected toe to bats any day of the week."

It was light enough by then to see around us. The pool was used by local women to do their wash.

Empty Clorox bottles littered the shore. I collected some discarded rags, torn but clean, and helped Susan bandage her foot. We took all the cloth we could find with us. The next part of the path, Susan said, would be rocky. When we got to it, we wrapped our feet as best we could in ropes of cotton. Not comfortable, but bearable. By eight o'clock we had reached the neck of the Princess, the dip between her chin and breast as she slept, face turned to the sky. In the distance lay the bold blue immensity of ocean.

Seeing the Pacific stretching across the whole horizon, acutely sensible suddenly of its power and its indifference, I despaired. With Dito gone I could see no hope for us. Whatever ties he had had with Noriega's Dignity Battalions, Georgie and Jardin would have the same connections. With Dito dead, Noriega's troops would be at their disposal, not his. Wherever we went, we would soon be picked up and delivered to our enemies. The way I saw it, we had no friends.

"Now what?" I growled.

"Well," said Susan, "now we get over to the road."

"Just like that!" I said sarcastically. The road she meant was on the opposite rim. We had another five mile trek ahead of us.

"Hey," she said, "you got a better idea, I'll be happy to do it."

Then I noticed that the rags on her left foot were red with blood. Ashamed, I said that I was sorry. I said, "Lead on."

We moved off down the path, each of us

immersed in private thoughts. I had been aware for some time that my ankles itched. I finally suggested that we sit a moment and rest. Susan sank to the ground. I sat beside her, took a look at my ankles and screamed. They were scaly with ticks.

"Leave them," Susan advised.

"Leave them! How can I leave them?"

"You better, you don't want their heads left. They'll infect. Frank's good at getting them out. Wait."

I wondered whether she really thought she would see Frank again. But I left the ticks to their breakfast and we went on. Susan was limping badly. My feet were sore and swollen and felt worse for having rested, but mine at least weren't cut. After a while I suggested to Susan that she put her arm around my neck, and she did.

We came upon a spring like the one at the base of Las Tres Hermanas where the square trees grow and the gold frogs used to live. We unwrapped our feet and bathed them. The red line emerging from Susan's wound was half an inch long. She worried the cut until it began to bleed again, a spiral of red dyeing the pool where she sat. I submerged my ankles. The water was cold enough to numb them, and I began surreptitiously picking at my freeloaders.

"You'll be sorry," said Susan.

"I already am," I replied shortly.

It was nearly ten o'clock and we hadn't yet run into anyone. I was fairly sure that by this time the word would be out about the two *gringas* wanted by the Dignity Battalions. I was afraid anyone we did

195

meet would be an enemy, would report having seen us, might even force us to accompany them, perhaps for a reward.

"How much further do you think it is to the road?"

"Oh not much," said Susan, then ruined it by adding, "I hope."

I told her my fear of meeting someone. She didn't seem surprised. "Did you have a plan?" I ventured. "When we get to the road?"

She pulled her lame foot out of the water and began to bind it again with the dirty rags.

"Wait!" I said, pulling off my blouse. I removed my undershirt and handed it to her. "Use this. It's cleaner."

"A plan," Susan muttered as she bound her foot. "A plan. Well, I just thought we'd get to the road and flag the first car. Have him take us to the nearest telephone."

I broke the silence by saying, "I guess that's all we can do."

"And hope for the best."

"Yeah. Hope for the best."

By now each step I took felt as if I were pummeling boils. Susan's arm around my neck weighed a ton. My head had begun to ache. I realized I was hungry, and tired as death.

I began to imagine what it would be like to be in a nice warm bath. The bath I imagined was one at Georgie's with the sweet smell of coral vine heavy in the air. I imagined drinking hot coffee from a mug, sipping orange juice, eating croissants with melon and proscuitto, in Georgie's kitchen. It was self-hypnosis and involuntary. On the kitchen table by the phantom basket of bread and croissants lay the photo album I had leafed through. I noticed again the empty spaces where Carlos's pictures once had been, the same pictures of Carlos that Bonifacio had shown me. In my mind I turned the pages of pictures once again and studied the faces of the many women there, beautiful women, some alone, some with their arms entwined with Georgie's, some nude, some of Georgie and another woman together nude, one with several women nude or nearly nude at the falls.

One had been familiar, and suddenly I remembered why. She was Guatemalan. Her name was Elena Calderon. She had been murdered in Panama several years before. *The New York Times* had reported that her murder had been ordered by a rival in their revolutionary faction. A few days later they reported that the rival had shot himself and the story dropped out of the news. As this memory surfaced from the depth of my subconscious I perceived for the first time a pattern to the events that had for so long seemed as unrelated as tangled spaghetti.

"For Christ's sake!" Susan said irritably. "What are you whistling for?"

"Was I whistling? I guess I just figured something out."

It was noon by the time we reached the road. For the last hour we had moved slowly through brush over the red volcanic soil on the Pacific side of the mountain. During that hour, I had pieced together most of the puzzle. It was more than intellectual satisfaction that buoyed my spirits, and lightened Susan's weight, for she had come to lean on me more and more.

We emerged from the sparse covering of brush about twenty yards below the surface of the road. A car stood parked on the narrow verge above us. Susan said, "What'll we do?"

"Chance it," I said.

The earth was shaley and difficult to manage. We climbed on all fours, like dogs, Susan first. I had to give her a boost from behind and, losing my grip, slid back a ways. Susan came out on the road a few feet behind the car. When I heard the car door slam and Susan start to scream, I was still too far down the slope to see what had happened.

My old pal, the Indian fellow with the long hair, was waiting for me on the road, gun in one hand, Susan in the other. Susan's arm was twisted painfully behind her back.

"You son of a bitch!" I yelled.

"Brigid, be careful, I'm okay, he'll shoot," Susan warned.

"I'm afraid she's right," said Georgie, her voice soft and controlled. I smelled her perfume the same instant I heard her voice. My stomach flipped over and with it the rosy-hued world I had been constructing in my mind for the past hour and a half.

"Let me give you a hand, kitten," said Georgie.

"Fuck off," said Brigid Donovan, girl detective. Brigid Donovan, hopeless romantic, hopeless sucker.

All the disgust I had felt toward Robert Jardin the night before rose in me like vomit. But now the object of my disgust was me.

I had managed to convince myself that Georgie had never betrayed me, that Georgie cared, that Georgie would rescue us now that Dito couldn't. But the neat little hole at the end of the Indian's gun had put a period to that fantasy.

"Brigid," said Georgie, "you're tired and upset. But be a dear and don't make trouble. Get in the car. You and Susan."

She shot off a rapid volley of Spanish to the Indian. He shrugged and let go of Susan, giving her a little shove so that she stumbled and fell. He pocketed his gun and ambled off down the hill.

I helped Susan to her feet. "Let's get out of here," she muttered in my ear.

"Don't be tiresome, Susan. You too, Brigid," said Georgie. She had opened the back door of the car. "Be dears, both of you, and get in."

It had begun to mist and a wind off the ocean had cooled the air considerably. A *bajareque* hid El Valle from view. Susan had started to shiver, her teeth chattering.

"I don't want you catching cold now, on top of everything else," Georgie said with motherly concern. "Brigid, wrap that blanket around her and you sit up front with me." I hesitated, and she added, "We have things to talk about . . . dear."

My traitor heart leaped into my throat. It drummed excitedly of hope, and like Jardin the night before, I meekly obeyed her.

Georgie drove down the winding road, passing the Indian who saluted us. At the first house, she turned the car around.

"Where's Robert?" I asked as we started back toward the valley.

"Let's wait," Georgie suggested, "until you've bathed and rested." She pointed at a thermos on the floor at my feet. "That coffee should be hot," she said. "I thought you might like some."

"How long had you been waiting for us?" I asked.

"Not long. An hour maybe."

It's hard to describe how depressed the whole thing made me. I said, "I guess we could have saved ourselves the hike."

"Oh no!" Georgie exclaimed. "Believe me, every blister and cut was well worth it for you. Your escape gave me time to do what needed to be done. I'll explain." She laid her hand on my thigh. "Later."

Susan's fit of coughing from the back seat sounded fake to me.

"Hello!" Georgie said. "I thought you had gone to sleep."

"No," said Susan. "I'm awake. Wide awake."

By the time I had finished bathing, soaking in hot water and scented oil for nearly an hour, and had wrapped myself in a voluminous terry-cloth robe which I found on the back of the bathroom door, Susan was sound asleep in bed. Really asleep, Georgie told me, as she tucked me in.

It was the same bed we had made love in, it seemed a lifetime ago. As Georgie bent over me, her silk robe fell open, and her breast, the nipple taut like a raspberry, appeared above my eye. Like a jacked deer, I stared until her low chuckle roused me and I began to babble.

"I cut my foot," I said. "It bled all over your rug."

"You broke my vase," said Georgie, deftly rearranging her robe and tying it. "I think cutting your foot served you right."

She had fed me before bringing me to bed. The melon of my fantasy, but no proscuitto. There had been croissants, though, and sweet butter, and Brie.

I said grumpily, nursing old grievances, "Bullshit! That was a terrible note you left me."

"It got you out of here."

"It nearly got me killed."

"Well," she said, "that was a miscalculation on my part." She kissed me lightly on the ear. "Actually," she said, "that note saved your life."

"A tree. A goddamned tree saved my life," I said petulantly.

She kissed my ear again. "Poor little kitten is all tired out. I'd get in bed with you, dear, but your cousin Susan said I was to leave you alone."

"Fuck my cousin Susan, too," I said, drifting off to sleep.

I slept for twelve hours, waking before dawn, waking about twenty-four hours after Susan and I had begun our long walk out of El Valle. Georgie was asleep beside me. I got up silently, careful not to wake her. It was cold and damp. I could hear the wind sough bleakly in the branches of the mango tree outside the window. My feet touched the terry-cloth robe lying on the floor where I had dropped it. I wrapped it around me. I didn't bother with the scuffs, quieter that way. I moved carefully, out the bedroom and down the hall to the French doors leading into the yard and the door to the cellar.

Someone had tidied up there. The crowbar had been replaced with the gardening tools. The surgical knife was back in the sterilizer. The bat cage, still empty, hung neatly from a nail. What I was looking for was on the gurney, a plain cardboard box. There were two boxes, actually. Dito's, and a new one, one I hadn't seen before. But I had expected to see it.

I dreaded confirming what I knew, what I had figured out on the trail, what then I had prayed for.

Jardin, unlike Dito, looked dismayed, unbelieving. I quickly closed the box again.

"Kitten, kitten! What are we going to do with you?" Georgie's voice behind me mocked. "You seem, dear, to have nine lives, but you really ought to think what curiosity does to kittens."

"Georgie," I said, "I'm going to be sick." I ran outside holding my mouth, the bile bitter in my throat. Under the mango tree, on the moist red soil, I knelt and vomited. Georgie came up behind me and held my head. She made soothing noises with her tongue.

"What are you going to do with them?" I asked when I was able.

"Do you have any good ideas?" she replied.

I turned and she hauled me to my feet. We stood silently a while watching the stars fade as the sky bleached a dirty gray. It began to rain again. "Come into the kitchen," she suggested. "We can talk there."

The coffee she made was good and strong, brewed in a sock. I took mine with sugar and cream.

"Dito's problem," she said, "was hubris. He couldn't take Jardin seriously. Never."

"When did you begin to?" I asked.

"I never trusted him," she shot back.

"Using him . . . ?"

"Was Dito's idea."

Georgie's mood was somber, her mind trapped in the maze of past events. But however much she retraced her steps, she always ended up in the present, at the nasty reality of those two boxes sitting side by side on the gurney in the cellar.

"Jardin must have loved you very much," I ventured.

"Love!" she spat. "I hate love."

The story was much as I had pieced it together, starting in Maine and ending with the insights I had gathered on the painful circumnavigation of the valley.

That long ago summer, confronted with her pregnancy, Georgie and Dito had taken advantage of Robert Jardin's adolescent passion. "It wasn't just me Robert was attracted to," said Georgie. "Not just sex. It was everything — class, power, the Hendryks name. Robert Jardin was ambitious."

"He adored you, Georgie."

"He was addicted to me!"

Her perspicacity surprised me; I had imagined her too vain to see it. For a moment Georgie's mood lightened, and she looked at me, laughing. I felt the heat of mortification dye my cheeks. "Poor kitten," said Georgie, covering my hand with hers to reassure me. "Sometimes I'm just all bad. You know," she confided, "he actually thought all those years that I was a virgin."

"Until Dito made that blunder at McLeod's."

"McLeod's?"

I told her about the dinner after Tony's funeral, with Clara, Robert Jardin, Dito and me. "When I mentioned Bonifacio, and Dito drew a blank, I thought it was his arrogance. How could Dito forget the mother of one of his own children, Carlos? Then, when he tried to cover up, I made another assumption, that you were the mother, and Robert Jardin the father. I thought, what a shocking way to discover someone was your son. And he started acting funny, Jardin. He left us there at the restaurant."

Georgie was amused anew. "Kitten, whatever would have made you think it was Robert Jardin who fathered my child?"

Except for blushing, I didn't take her bait. I said, "There was a rumor in the valley that summer. Some North Koreans hanging out at your place? I checked it out. The only subversive sort I ever saw was Robert Jardin. Also, you were engaged to him. For a while."

"Poor Robert," she murmured.

When Georgie's interest in women became common gossip and Jardin could no longer pretend he didn't know, he seemed to accept gracefully the fact that Georgie would never marry him.

"For a long time he seemed to be content, as if somehow so long as I never married, and he didn't, we could spend our lives in his adolescent fantasy."

"When did the drugs start?" I asked.

Georgie sighed. She ran her fingers through her short curly hair. "You want more coffee?" she asked.

"What I really want are answers, Georgie."

"Okay," she said resignedly. "I guess you deserve a few."

About ten or twelve years before, not long after the Reagan Administration's war on Central America began, Jardin had come to Georgie and Dito with a proposition. He offered to cut them into a burgeoning drugs-for-arms trade being organized and protected by the CIA.

"Something about the Clark amendment, Congress couldn't support these covert operations any more. Then there was the bombing of Corinto harbor and the CIA was on the spot for that. So, they still wanted to arm the Contras. Then they hit on the idea of, well, what it amounted to was organizing the cocaine trade. Jardin offered to let us in on the ground floor."

"Why did you do it?"

"Why? Why not?"

"Georgie! That's terrible."

"Nonsense! The market had fallen out of Colombian coffee. Our people weren't making it. Do you remember what it was like in Colombia in nineteen-eighty? The political bombings, the kidnappings? It was no longer civilized. And people were dying. Dying of hunger."

"Oh yeah," I said. "It was so much worse then than it is now. The fact of the matter is, you and Dito made a killing. And you made it by using Robert Jardin. When did it start to sour?"

"You always were a prig, Brigid. You know that?"

"Tell me. How many of your girlfriends did he kill before you began to get worried?"

She looked surprised and I found that gratifying.

"How did you know?"

"I recognized the picture of Elena Calderon," I said. "I got to wondering how many others of those women in the album had met a violent end."

"Three," she said, looking for the first time downcast.

"Only three?"

She brightened a little. "I believe you might have been the fourth, kitten."

"Thanks a lot."

She said that when I had appeared on her doorstep that day she was completely taken aback. "Jardin had called to say you would be coming. I tried to divert you. It wasn't easy fixing that album. Bonifacio couldn't write very well."

"Why did you bother?" I asked.

"I was afraid for you." She reached across and pinched my cheek. "Little kitten. I'm fond of you. I knew by then that Jardin was a psychopath."

"Why," I asked, "would he want to hurt me? I hardly knew him."

"But it's what you said. He had three of my lovers killed. He knew I was fond of you."

"How could he know that?" I asked, increasingly skeptical of her explanations.

"Ah, kitten, kitten. I was only waiting for you to grow up. But then you went into the convent. I wanted to be the one to bring you out. Instead it was some nun, I bet. Which one was it? Sr. Anne? Sr. Marguerite?"

"Who brought *you* out?" I asked. If she had said

Sr. Anne, I would have killed her on the spot. Figured I could have found one more cardboard box somewhere.

"Oh, neither of them. Don't upset yourself. She was a senior from Chicago. We still write."

I considered what she had told me. When she asked again whether I wanted another cup of coffee, I agreed, somewhat absent-mindedly. While she fussed at the sink, rinsing the sock, measuring the coffee, I asked more questions.

"You were afraid Jardin would have me killed if I slept with you?"

"Mmmm," she said.

"Then why did you do it?"

"Oh now, Brigid, don't go offending an old lady. I thought you wanted to go to bed with me."

My throat went dry with remembered desire. "Yeah," I muttered.

Georgie pulled her chair up close to mine and took my hand in both of hers. "Brigid, dear, what I did was foolish and I hope you can forgive me. But I couldn't resist the temptation. For years I had wanted to take this darling little girl to bed with me, and then there she was suddenly, on my doorstep."

In the early morning light, Georgie's eyes gleamed with humor as she said, "With her tongue hanging out. After all those years."

"Oh, stop!" I said and jerked my hand free.

"Seriously, I thought it would be all right. I had called Jardin and told him that Bonifacio had talked with you and that I believed you were on your way back to the States. I thought if I got you right out of here in the morning, no one would be the wiser. I was wrong. Arnulfo had instructions — I didn't know it at the time — to get rid of you if you spent the night." She looked at me thoughtfully and then said, "Part of the problem was your confiding in Jardin. I could never understand why you seemed to trust him."

How could I tell this woman that trusting Jardin was my way of being able to trust Clara? I didn't need to.

"Of course," said Georgie, "you wanted to believe in Sr. Clara. Poor kitten. Robert told me about your infatuation."

"Yeah," I said, ignoring the infatuation part. "What's going to happen to her?"

"What do you mean, what's going to happen to her?"

"Won't she go to jail?"

"Jail? Oh, no. Jardin wasn't running drugs through Monte Cassino."

Jardin, it seemed, had been making his donations to Clara to provide a red herring, to divert attention from the Coast Guard Station through which the drugs really did flow. Georgie said, "What Clara got was only small potatoes."

"Not so small," I amended. "Sr. Barnabas got a share."

The rest of Georgie's story was what I had already figured out. Craziness, jealousy, and the power to do it, had driven Jardin to begin eliminating all the rivals he perceived for Georgie's affections. Carlos, two years before, had been his first hit.

"Robert knew how I doted on Carlos. Besides,

Carlos was determined to queer Robert's little operation there in Maine."

"I thought Maria killed Carlos. By accident."

"Well," Georgie said, consideringly. "Accidents don't always just happen. Jardin set that one up. I think he intended for them both to die, Maria and Carlos. But that storm blew up. Someone, I forget his name . . ."

"Rollie."

"Right. I think Jardin intended to have Rollie get rid of them both, there on the island. There's a cedar bog?"

"That's right. If you knew all this . . ."

"Why didn't I stop it? I only just found out about it."

"Last night?"

She nodded. "Before he died. He told me many things. He said he had just found out how Dito had "ravished me". He told me that was why Dito had had to die. Because of Carlos. He told me not to worry. He said Noriega would be blamed. That he could see to that. Just like Spadaforo."

"What about Tony?" I asked. "Was his death an accident?"

"Poor Tony," she sighed. "An accident. Not at all. It really all began with Tony. As Dito groomed Tony to take our place, mine and Dito's, Jardin seemed to get funny, resentful. I'm sure he's the one who got Tony into drugs. And I believe it was Jardin who supplied the drugs that killed him."

It was all so nice and pat and I wanted desperately to believe it. All of it. "What happened?" I asked. "To Jardin?"

"Oh, kitten," she said wearily. "What do you want me to tell you?"

"The truth. What happened. God, Georgie, how could you have done that to him?"

"How could I do to him what he did to Dito? Well, as a matter of fact I didn't. That maniac Arnulfo took care of Robert."

"Don't split hairs. You ordered it."

"Well," she temporized. "What I told Arnulfo was that Jardin intended to turn him over to Noriega. I said, 'Do whatever you think best.' I did suggest that he do to Jardin whatever it was Jardin had ordered done to the two ladies when they were found."

That shut me up.

We kept silence for a while. I became conscious of birds singing gaily. I envied them their innocence.

"Georgie, what about the bats?"

"What about them?"

"Well, whose idea were they?"

"Oh," she said, and brusquely pushed some air aside. "Nobody's. I told Benito, that is Bonifacio's son, to scare you. I don't know what made him think of bats."

"It was pretty effective," I said. "Especially the cage of bats in the cellar. That Benito's idea too?"

"Oh that," she said, modestly.

"Why was Bonifacio killed?"

"Same as the others."

"You mean . . ." Something like jealousy kept me from finishing the thought.

"No, no. Not for a long time. But we were close, good friends." She sighed. "When Bonifacio died, I knew he had to be stopped. There was no possibility of coincidence any more. But you couldn't talk to

Dito. Hubris. He just refused to take Robert seriously. Even after Robert found out about us, about Carlos, that Carlos was our child, Dito's and mine."

I thought about it all in silence for a while. Georgie began to clear the table. The sun warmed my face. I could smell the coral vine. It felt good to be alive. "What happens next?" I asked.

"Next," Georgie said energetically, "we get you back to Maine and Susan back to Curundu and Frank."

"My God! Frank! Does he know . . ."

"That you're both okay? Yes. In fact I expect him here any moment. He'll take *you* directly to Tocumen. You have a reservation straight through to Bangor. Maybe we should wake Susan up."

"Susan's awake," said Susan, yawning in the doorway.

"How does your foot feel?" I asked.

"Not as nice as her hands, I bet," said Georgie. "But we could ask Frank about that. There he is at the door now."

Chapter 13

I left Panama on the nineteenth of December.
The U.S. invasion began an hour or so after I
landed in Bangor. There never was a report, in the
long list of Noriega's crimes, that he had beheaded a
CIA man named Robert Jardin, or a Panamanian
crony named Orlando (Dito) Brown. The word in
Blue Hill was that Robert Jardin had disappeared.
Some people were reminded of "that fellah with the
INS, the one that up and disappeared a few years
back. What was his name . . . Brown. Carlos Brown.

Something like that." Some said Robert Jardin had had a sweetheart in one of them Banana Republics and run off with her. Later, when I heard about the mass graves in Panama, I decided Georgie, or Arnulfo, had made use of one to dispose of the bodies, Dito's and Jardin's.

As news of what had really occurred began to come through, I worried about what had happened to Ed, my taxi driver. To him and his wife, and all those others I had seen that morning on the streets of Chorrillo. I worried, too, about Bonifacio's son, and her grandson, in San Miguelito. Both barrios had been destroyed, bombed and burned.

At the new year, Georgie came to Blue Hill to visit. She stayed with Clara on Monte Cassino, and I got the impression that Katie the cow hadn't had to make room in the manger for Clara. By the time Georgie left, on Valentine's Day, she had bankrolled something for refugees called Bethany International, and had made Clara the head. Bethany because that's where Jesus stayed when he preached his Sermon on the Mount. Clara said she was inspired that through humbleness she would inherit the kingdom. Any kingdom, I guess, would do.

Georgie generally spread her largess. She supplemented Maria's income until Carlos could be declared legally dead. And she gave Alex a ticket to Arizona. One way. That, she said, was "for you, kitten." I said nonsense, Sr. Pat was already married, to Jesus. Georgie said I should never let that get in my way.

As it turned out, I was the one to take Alex to the airport. I told her she should send her manuscript, *Only One Thing in This Book Is True: I Never Read Thoreau,* to Naiad Press. When she asked did I like the title, I told her it was different.

Bruce took full credit for stopping the flow of drugs from Canada into Maine.

After Alex left, Pat suggested that I spend the winter in the convent. Said I'd think about it. I still do.

A few of the publications of
THE NAIAD PRESS, INC.
P.O. Box 10543 • Tallahassee, Florida 32302
Phone (904) 539-5965
Mail orders welcome. Please include 15% postage.

MURDER IS GERMANE by Karen Saum. 224 pp. The 2nd
Brigid Donovan mystery. ISBN 0-941483-98-3 $8.95

TO LOVE AGAIN by Evelyn Kennedy. 208 pp. Wildly
romantic love story. ISBN 0-941483-85-1 9.95

IN THE GAME by Nikki Baker. 192 pp. A Virginia Kelly
mystery. First in a series. ISBN 01-56280-004-3 8.95

AVALON by Mary Jane Jones. 256 pp. A Lesbian Arthurian
romance. ISBN 0-941483-96-7 9.95

STRANDED by Camarin Grae. 320 pp. Entertaining, riveting
adventure. ISBN 0-941483-99-1 9.95

THE DAUGHTERS OF ARTEMIS by Lauren Wright Douglas.
240 pp. Third Caitlin Reece mystery. ISBN 0-941483-95-9 8.95

CLEARWATER by Catherine Ennis. 176 pp. Romantic secrets
of a small Louisiana town. ISBN 0-941483-65-7 8.95

THE HALLELUJAH MURDERS by Dorothy Tell. 176 pp.
Second Poppy Dillworth mystery. ISBN 0-941483-88-6 8.95

ZETA BASE by Judith Alguire. 208 pp. Lesbian triangle
on a future Earth. ISBN 0-941483-94-0 9.95

SECOND CHANCE by Jackie Calhoun. 256 pp. Contemporary
Lesbian lives and loves. ISBN 0-941483-93-2 9.95

MURDER BY TRADITION by Katherine V. Forrest. 288 pp.
A Kate Delafield Mystery. 4th in a series. ISBN 0-941483-89-4 18.95

BENEDICTION by Diane Salvatore. 272 pp. Striking,
contemporary romantic novel. ISBN 0-941483-90-8 9.95

CALLING RAIN by Karen Marie Christa Minns. 240 pp.
Spellbinding, erotic love story ISBN 0-941483-87-8 9.95

BLACK IRIS by Jeane Harris. 192 pp. Caroline's hidden past . . .
 ISBN 0-941483-68-1 8.95

TOUCHWOOD by Karin Kallmaker. 240 pp. Loving, May/
December romance. ISBN 0-941483-76-2 8.95

BAYOU CITY SECRETS by Deborah Powell. 224 pp. A Hollis
Carpenter mystery. First in a series. ISBN 0-941483-91-6 8.95

COP OUT by Claire McNab. 208 pp. 4th Det. Insp. Carol Ashton
mystery. ISBN 0-941483-84-3 8.95

LODESTAR by Phyllis Horn. 224 pp. Romantic, fast-moving
adventure.   ISBN 0-941483-83-5   8.95

THE BEVERLY MALIBU by Katherine V. Forrest. 288 pp. A
Kate Delafield Mystery. 3rd in a series. (HC) ISBN 0-941483-47-9   16.95
                        Paperback ISBN 0-941483-48-7   9.95

THAT OLD STUDEBAKER by Lee Lynch. 272 pp. Andy's affair
with Regina and her attachment to her beloved car.
                                        ISBN 0-941483-82-7   9.95

PASSION'S LEGACY by Lori Paige. 224 pp. Sarah is swept into
the arms of Augusta Pym in this delightful historical romance.
                                        ISBN 0-941483-81-9   8.95

THE PROVIDENCE FILE by Amanda Kyle Williams. 256 pp.
Second espionage thriller featuring lesbian agent Madison McGuire
                                        ISBN 0-941483-92-4   8.95

I LEFT MY HEART by Jaye Maiman. 320 pp. A Robin Miller
Mystery. First in a series.   ISBN 0-941483-72-X   9.95

THE PRICE OF SALT by Patricia Highsmith (writing as Claire
Morgan). 288 pp. Classic lesbian novel, first issued in 1952 . . .
acknowledged by its author under her own, very famous, name.
                                        ISBN 1-56280-003-5   8.95

SIDE BY SIDE by Isabel Miller. 256 pp. From beloved author of
Patience and Sarah.   ISBN 0-941483-77-0   8.95

SOUTHBOUND by Sheila Ortiz Taylor. 240 pp. Hilarious sequel
to *Faultline.*   ISBN 0-941483-78-9   8.95

STAYING POWER: LONG TERM LESBIAN COUPLES
by Susan E. Johnson. 352 pp. Joys of coupledom.
                                        ISBN 0-941-483-75-4   12.95

SLICK by Camarin Grae. 304 pp. Exotic, erotic adventure.
                                        ISBN 0-941483-74-6   9.95

NINTH LIFE by Lauren Wright Douglas. 256 pp. A Caitlin
Reece mystery. 2nd in a series.   ISBN 0-941483-50-9   8.95

PLAYERS by Robbi Sommers. 192 pp. Sizzling, erotic novel.
                                        ISBN 0-941483-73-8   8.95

MURDER AT RED ROOK RANCH by Dorothy Tell. 224 pp.
First Poppy Dillworth adventure.   ISBN 0-941483-80-0   8.95

LESBIAN SURVIVAL MANUAL by Rhonda Dicksion.
112 pp. Cartoons!   ISBN 0-941483-71-1   8.95

A ROOM FULL OF WOMEN by Elisabeth Nonas. 256 pp.
Contemporary Lesbian lives.   ISBN 0-941483-69-X   8.95

MURDER IS RELATIVE by Karen Saum. 256 pp. The first
Brigid Donovan mystery.   ISBN 0-941483-70-3   8.95

PRIORITIES by Lynda Lyons 288 pp. Science fiction with
a twist.   ISBN 0-941483-66-5   8.95

THEME FOR DIVERSE INSTRUMENTS by Jane Rule. 208
pp. Powerful romantic lesbian stories.   ISBN 0-941483-63-0   8.95

LESBIAN QUERIES by Hertz & Ertman. 112 pp. The questions
you were too embarrassed to ask.   ISBN 0-941483-67-3   8.95

CLUB 12 by Amanda Kyle Williams. 288 pp. Espionage thriller
featuring a lesbian agent!   ISBN 0-941483-64-9   8.95

DEATH DOWN UNDER by Claire McNab. 240 pp. 3rd Det.
Insp. Carol Ashton mystery.   ISBN 0-941483-39-8   8.95

MONTANA FEATHERS by Penny Hayes. 256 pp. Vivian and
Elizabeth find love in frontier Montana.   ISBN 0-941483-61-4   8.95

CHESAPEAKE PROJECT by Phyllis Horn. 304 pp. Jessie &
Meredith in perilous adventure.   ISBN 0-941483-58-4   8.95

LIFESTYLES by Jackie Calhoun. 224 pp. Contemporary Lesbian
lives and loves.   ISBN 0-941483-57-6   8.95

VIRAGO by Karen Marie Christa Minns. 208 pp. Darsen has
chosen Ginny.   ISBN 0-941483-56-8   8.95

WILDERNESS TREK by Dorothy Tell. 192 pp. Six women on
vacation learning "new" skills.   ISBN 0-941483-60-6   8.95

MURDER BY THE BOOK by Pat Welch. 256 pp. A Helen
Black Mystery. First in a series.   ISBN 0-941483-59-2   8.95

BERRIGAN by Vicki P. McConnell. 176 pp. Youthful Lesbian —
romantic, idealistic Berrigan.   ISBN 0-941483-55-X   8.95

LESBIANS IN GERMANY by Lillian Faderman & B. Eriksson.
128 pp. Fiction, poetry, essays.   ISBN 0-941483-62-2   8.95

THERE'S SOMETHING I'VE BEEN MEANING TO TELL
YOU Ed. by Loralee MacPike. 288 pp. Gay men and lesbians
coming out to their children.   ISBN 0-941483-44-4   9.95
                                       ISBN 0-941483-54-1   16.95

LIFTING BELLY by Gertrude Stein. Ed. by Rebecca Mark. 104
pp. Erotic poetry.   ISBN 0-941483-51-7   8.95
                            ISBN 0-941483-53-3   14.95

ROSE PENSKI by Roz Perry. 192 pp. Adult lovers in a long-term
relationship.   ISBN 0-941483-37-1   8.95

AFTER THE FIRE by Jane Rule. 256 pp. Warm, human novel
by this incomparable author.   ISBN 0-941483-45-2   8.95

SUE SLATE, PRIVATE EYE by Lee Lynch. 176 pp. The gay
folk of Peacock Alley are all cats.   ISBN 0-941483-52-5   8.95

CHRIS by Randy Salem. 224 pp. Golden oldie. Handsome Chris
and her adventures.   ISBN 0-941483-42-8   8.95

THREE WOMEN by March Hastings. 232 pp. Golden oldie. A
triangle among wealthy sophisticates.   ISBN 0-941483-43-6   8.95

HIGH CONTRAST by Jessie Lattimore. 264 pp. Women of the
Crystal Palace. ISBN 0-941483-17-7   8.95

OCTOBER OBSESSION by Meredith More. Josie's rich, secret
Lesbian life. ISBN 0-941483-18-5   8.95

LESBIAN CROSSROADS by Ruth Baetz. 276 pp. Contemporary
Lesbian lives. ISBN 0-941483-21-5   9.95

BEFORE STONEWALL: THE MAKING OF A GAY AND
LESBIAN COMMUNITY by Andrea Weiss & Greta Schiller.
96 pp., 25 illus. ISBN 0-941483-20-7   7.95

WE WALK THE BACK OF THE TIGER by Patricia A. Murphy.
192 pp. Romantic Lesbian novel/beginning women's movement.
ISBN 0-941483-13-4   8.95

SUNDAY'S CHILD by Joyce Bright. 216 pp. Lesbian athletics, at
last the novel about sports. ISBN 0-941483-12-6   8.95

OSTEN'S BAY by Zenobia N. Vole. 204 pp. Sizzling adventure
romance set on Bonaire. ISBN 0-941483-15-0   8.95

LESSONS IN MURDER by Claire McNab. 216 pp. 1st Det. Inspec.
Carol Ashton mystery — erotic tension!. ISBN 0-941483-14-2   8.95

YELLOWTHROAT by Penny Hayes. 240 pp. Margarita, bandit,
kidnaps Julia. ISBN 0-941483-10-X   8.95

SAPPHISTRY: THE BOOK OF LESBIAN SEXUALITY by
Pat Califia. 3d edition, revised. 208 pp. ISBN 0-941483-24-X   8.95

CHERISHED LOVE by Evelyn Kennedy. 192 pp. Erotic
Lesbian love story. ISBN 0-941483-08-8   8.95

LAST SEPTEMBER by Helen R. Hull. 208 pp. Six stories & a
glorious novella. ISBN 0-941483-09-6   8.95

THE SECRET IN THE BIRD by Camarin Grae. 312 pp. Striking,
psychological suspense novel. ISBN 0-941483-05-3   8.95

TO THE LIGHTNING by Catherine Ennis. 208 pp. Romantic
Lesbian 'Robinson Crusoe' adventure. ISBN 0-941483-06-1   8.95

THE OTHER SIDE OF VENUS by Shirley Verel. 224 pp.
Luminous, romantic love story. ISBN 0-941483-07-X   8.95

DREAMS AND SWORDS by Katherine V. Forrest. 192 pp.
Romantic, erotic, imaginative stories. ISBN 0-941483-03-7   8.95

MEMORY BOARD by Jane Rule. 336 pp. Memorable novel
about an aging Lesbian couple. ISBN 0-941483-02-9   9.95

THE ALWAYS ANONYMOUS BEAST by Lauren Wright
Douglas. 224 pp. A Caitlin Reece mystery. First in a series.
ISBN 0-941483-04-5   8.95

SEARCHING FOR SPRING by Patricia A. Murphy. 224 pp.
Novel about the recovery of love. ISBN 0-941483-00-2   8.95

DUSTY'S QUEEN OF HEARTS DINER by Lee Lynch. 240 pp.
Romantic blue-collar novel.   ISBN 0-941483-01-0   8.95

PARENTS MATTER by Ann Muller. 240 pp. Parents'
relationships with Lesbian daughters and gay sons.
                                               ISBN 0-930044-91-6   9.95

THE PEARLS by Shelley Smith. 176 pp. Passion and fun in
the Caribbean sun.   ISBN 0-930044-93-2   7.95

MAGDALENA by Sarah Aldridge. 352 pp. Epic Lesbian novel
set on three continents.   ISBN 0-930044-99-1   8.95

THE BLACK AND WHITE OF IT by Ann Allen Shockley.
144 pp. Short stories.   ISBN 0-930044-96-7   7.95

SAY JESUS AND COME TO ME by Ann Allen Shockley. 288
pp. Contemporary romance.   ISBN 0-930044-98-3   8.95

LOVING HER by Ann Allen Shockley. 192 pp. Romantic love
story.   ISBN 0-930044-97-5   7.95

MURDER AT THE NIGHTWOOD BAR by Katherine V.
Forrest. 240 pp. A Kate Delafield mystery. Second in a series.
                                               ISBN 0-930044-92-4   9.95

ZOE'S BOOK by Gail Pass. 224 pp. Passionate, obsessive love
story.   ISBN 0-930044-95-9   7.95

WINGED DANCER by Camarin Grae. 228 pp. Erotic Lesbian
adventure story.   ISBN 0-930044-88-6   8.95

PAZ by Camarin Grae. 336 pp. Romantic Lesbian adventurer
with the power to change the world.   ISBN 0-930044-89-4   8.95

SOUL SNATCHER by Camarin Grae. 224 pp. A puzzle, an
adventure, a mystery — Lesbian romance.   ISBN 0-930044-90-8   8.95

THE LOVE OF GOOD WOMEN by Isabel Miller. 224 pp.
Long-awaited new novel by the author of the beloved *Patience
and Sarah.*   ISBN 0-930044-81-9   8.95

THE HOUSE AT PELHAM FALLS by Brenda Weathers. 240
pp. Suspenseful Lesbian ghost story.   ISBN 0-930044-79-7   7.95

HOME IN YOUR HANDS by Lee Lynch. 240 pp. More stories
from the author of *Old Dyke Tales.*   ISBN 0-930044-80-0   7.95

EACH HAND A MAP by Anita Skeen. 112 pp. Real-life poems
that touch us all.   ISBN 0-930044-82-7   6.95

These are just a few of the many Naiad Press titles — we are the oldest and
largest lesbian/feminist publishing company in the world. Please request a
complete catalog. We offer personal service; we encourage and welcome direct
mail orders from individuals who have limited access to bookstores carrying
our publications.